THE ROGUE WARRIOR

NAVY SEAL ROMANCES 2.0

CINDY ROLAND ANDERSON

WINSOME
PRESS
PUBLISHING

Line Editor: Sadie L Anderson

Content Editor: Valerie Bybee

Cover Design by Valerie Bybee Photography

Cover Photo by Valerie Bybee Photography

Cover Model: Trevor Farnes

❀ Created with Vellum

For the men and women serving in the United States Armed Forces, selflessly protecting our freedom and sometimes giving their lives for it. Thank you so much!

CHAPTER 1

$\mathcal{F}$reedom. For the first time in months, she felt liberated from the grief that had entrapped her for so long. Tipping her face up, Weslee Campbell closed her eyes and listened to the sound of the crashing waves as a soft ocean breeze caressed her face. It felt as if her mama was reaching down from heaven to stroke her cheek.

"I miss you," she whispered. "But I'm ready to start living again."

Opening her eyes, she stared across the vast ocean. The setting sun created a spectacular skyline of amber light that shimmered on the surface of the water. A small smile tipped her mouth as she remembered how her daddy would always take dozens of pictures, trying to capture the array of colors. He never could get it right, but that didn't matter because he told her that God would give them another sunset tomorrow.

Thinking about her parents made her ache with longing to see them again, but the pain wasn't as raw. She knew they wouldn't want her to grieve so deeply anymore. Coming to

San Diego had been the right thing to do. Her parents had loved visiting the West Coast.

A wave rolled over the beach, nearly touching her bare feet. Weslee curled her toes into the moist sand, welcoming the sensations as if she had never experienced them before. When her parents had died in a car accident eight months earlier, Weslee didn't know if she would ever want to step foot on another beach.

Growing up in a quiet suburb of Raleigh, North Carolina, she and her parents spent most of the weekends in their beach house on Emerald Isle. The long stretch of the North Carolina private beach provided the perfect getaway for their small family. It's where Weslee learned how to swim, fish, and shoot arrows. She hadn't been able to bring herself to visit the Emerald Isle home. It was the last place they'd all been together. But the oceanfront house in San Diego was a good first step back into life. Her parents made the trip out west at least once a month. This would be the first year they wouldn't attend the annual charity ball held at the historic Hotel del Coronado. The invitation had come a few weeks after their funeral. Weslee had almost tossed it in the trash. Thank goodness Inez, her childhood nanny and now housekeeper, had tucked it away.

The sound of laughter drew her attention away from the rolling water. She watched the party of teenagers playing volleyball, tempting her to ask if she could join them. She hadn't wanted to do anything social for so long. Was she brave enough to venture closer?

Her phone pinged an incoming text. She pulled it from the pocket of her white sundress and froze as she read the first few lines previewed on the screen. Her throat closed off as she frantically looked around her. Was he watching her right now? And how had he gotten her new number?

Fingers shaking, she tapped on the message. She had really hoped the guy was going to leave her alone since he hadn't contacted her for two weeks. All of them had hoped her stalker had lost interest. But following her to California crossed a line. Angry and frustrated, she read the entire text.

You look real pretty in your white dress. I wish your hair wasn't braided so I could watch it dance on the breeze.

He really was here. Feeling as exposed as a deer during hunting season, she tried to pull up the keypad to call 9-1-1 but her hands shook and her fingers felt frozen. Deciding to seek shelter first, she shoved the phone back into her pocket and spun around to run back to the house. She caught sight of a dark shirt just before she slammed into something hard.

A scream pierced the air as she fell on her backside. Her eyes widened with fear as she looked up to see the muscular man she'd hit. "Stay away from me," she said, scrambling backward like one of the sand crabs.

"Easy," the man said, holding up his hands in surrender. "I didn't mean to run into you."

"You...you need to stop contacting me."

Confusion darkened his features, his blue eyes narrowing. "Ma'am, I think you may have me confused with someone else." He emphasized his empty hands. "I protect women, not hurt them."

"You're a police officer?" she asked, feeling as if he had just put up an invisible force field around her. For whatever reason, she believed him and knew he wasn't the man stalking her.

"No, ma'am. I'm an officer...a recently retired officer in the Navy." He scanned the area around them. "Is there someone here who threatened you?"

"I don't know if he's here or not." Weslee's racing heartbeat began to slow down as she got to her feet. "He texted me a minute ago and described my dress," she said, shivering at the thought that her stalker was still watching her.

The lines in his face hardened as he made another slow sweep of their surroundings. Weslee scanned the area too. With someone like this Navy guy here to protect her, now would be the perfect time to spot the man sending her the messages. She didn't see anyone suspicious.

Glancing back at the naval officer, she waited as he continued his thorough search of their immediate landscape. He looked far too young for retirement. She had just turned twenty-five, and he had to be close to her age or only a few years older.

Her eyes zeroed in on an insignia visible on the sleeve of his blue T-shirt. She wasn't sure what it said, but it looked legit. Her eyes drifted down to his well-developed bicep that strained against the fabric of his snug shirt. She was confident this man could protect her.

His hands were on his hips as he continued to search the area. That's when she noticed two bracelets made from thin black cord circled one of his wrists. They were definitely homemade. She'd made that kind of friendship bracelet at a few of the summer camps she'd attended when she was a little girl. Maybe he had a daughter or a little sister who had made them for him.

"Ma'am, I don't see anyone."

Weslee jerked her head up. "Oh…okay."

"Would you like me to call the police?"

"No, thank you." She didn't want to bother the local police, doubting they could do anything more than the police back home. "I'll contact the detective working with me."

Their gazes held, the air between them charged with electricity. His blue eyes assessed her with the same intensity as when he'd searched for her stalker. It wasn't exactly uncomfortable or creepy, just intense as if he were puzzling over an equation.

She was on the verge of asking for his name when Inez called out from behind her. "Baby girl, are you okay?" she asked, her wobbly voice a sign of her worry.

"Yes, ma'am," Weslee said, breaking eye contact with her Navy rescuer. Inez was coming toward her, limping slightly from her arthritic knees. Weslee needed to go to her, knowing the older woman would risk further damage to make sure she was safe. Besides, she needed to contact Uncle Jon and tell him about the text message.

"Thank you again for your help," she said, pushing a loose strand of hair behind her ear. "I really appreciate it."

He still watched her closely and, for a moment, she thought he would ask for her contact information. Part of her wished he would. Then she reminded herself she lived on the East Coast and that she was leaving after the charity ball next weekend. There was no point in even knowing his name.

The muscle in his jaw tightened as something decisive flickered in his eyes. "No problem, ma'am," he said, giving her a nod of his chin.

With his dismissal, Weslee gave him a soft smile before she turned and walked away. She wanted to look behind her one last time, but Inez stumbled and nearly went down. "Don't come any further," she said, picking up her pace. "I'm comin' to you."

"Who is that young man?" Inez asked when Weslee was almost to her.

"I don't know his name." Weslee reached Inez and took her arm. "I accidentally ran into him."

"Accidentally on purpose?" Inez asked, her eyes sparkling with amusement. "Even from here I could see he was a handsome devil."

Was? Unable to help herself, Weslee glanced behind her. Mr. Navy had resumed his jog, heading back in the direction he'd come from. It was silly to feel so disappointed. "He was very handsome," Weslee said. "And I think he would've taken out my stalker if he had found him."

Inez stopped so abruptly they both nearly tumbled to the ground. "That man is here?"

"I think so." Weslee took the older woman's hand in hers and escorted her up the wooden stairs to the covered porch. "He knew the color of my dress and that my hair is braided."

"We have to tell Jon," Inez said. "Promise me you'll do what he asks this time?"

"I promise," she said, although reluctantly. Jon would insist on hiring a bodyguard. He'd wanted to before. But, since the messages were never threatening, Weslee had talked him out of it. She didn't want to have some huge man following her around. "But I'm not missing the charity ball."

"Then make sure Jon hires someone who can dance," Inez said, narrowing her eyes. "The important thing is to keep you safe."

She shivered at the serious tone of her former nanny's words. Would this man hurt her? While this message was similar to the others, talking about her clothes and her hair, the fact he'd followed her to California was alarming. That, and the recent disappearances of two college girls from Duke University who had both received messages from an unknown admirer before they went missing caused another shiver of fear to snake down her spine. They were too similar to her case.

Once inside, Weslee made the call to her uncle. Jon Curtis wasn't really her uncle. He was her father's best friend and the corporate attorney for Ground Zero, the nutritional supplement company her daddy had built into a multi-million-dollar company from the ground up. Weslee had known Jon all her life. Since both of her parents had no other living relatives, he and Inez were her only family.

"Hello, Weslee my girl," Jon answered cheerfully. "Have you had a good day?"

"Yes." She sank down on an oversized white leather chair. "At least I was until I got another message from my overzealous fan."

Jon exploded after Weslee read him the text. "Did you call the police?"

"No. They can't do anything with a single text message."

"I'll be on the plane within the hour. In the meantime, I'll call in a favor with a colleague of mine. He has connections with an exclusive security firm based out of San Diego." Jon went on to give her other instructions, like making sure she closed all the blinds, locked the doors, and armed the security system. He also promised to have a police officer watch over the house until he could arrange for a bodyguard. Weslee didn't argue. Jon rarely overreacted, but this time he'd sounded panicked.

After ending the call, she made sure to lock all the doors and closed the blinds. This whole thing angered her. She didn't want a bodyguard, and she didn't want to be sequestered in the house. She loved the view of the ocean and felt frustrated that she couldn't keep the blinds open because some guy had decided to fixate on her.

Still, she wasn't exactly safe with a crazy stalker who wanted to be close enough he could touch her hair. He mentioned something about it in every single message. It was kind of creepy how obsessed the guy was about her hair. It's not like it was anything extraordinary. She was blonde with natural beach waves that came to the middle of her back. He also commented on her clothing and how well everything fit her. That was creepy too, now that she thought about it.

"Here you go, sugar," Inez said, handing Weslee a steaming cup of cocoa. The big dollop of whipped cream was already melting into a white puddle.

"Thank you." She blew across the top before taking a sip. "This is exactly what I needed."

"What did Jon say?" Inez asked, sitting on a matching chair next to Weslee.

"He's on his way out." Weslee took another sip of cocoa and winced. It was still a little too hot. "And he's hiring a bodyguard to follow me around."

"It won't be that bad." She picked up her knitting bag and pulled out her latest project. "Did you ask Jon to make sure he hires someone who is handsome and can dance?"

"No. Somehow I don't think Jon will take that into consideration." Weslee lowered the cup to her lap. "He'll go for someone who looks like the bodyguards in the movies with big muscles, sunglasses, and zero personality."

A smile crinkled the corners of Inez's eyes. "That's going to put a damper on all those handsome young men wanting to dance with you Saturday evening."

"Or he could rescue me from being a wallflower if no one else asks me to dance."

Her nanny snorted a laugh. "Honey, you have never in your life been a wallflower."

"I have too," Weslee argued. "Don't you remember my eighth-grade dance? Not one single boy asked me to dance."

"That's because that mean girl, Lillianna Carlton, paid them off."

Lillianna Carlton had been the bane of Weslee's existence up until high school. Her tormentor had gotten pregnant the beginning of their sophomore year, freeing Weslee from her incessant harassment. "I think she lives out here and is on husband number three." Weslee sipped her cocoa and then licked the cream from her upper lip. "I hope she isn't at the charity ball."

"Well, you've got more money than her now, so you can pay all the men more than five dollars not to dance with her."

"Hmm, remind me to bring a lot of cash with me."

Her phone chimed an incoming text. She and Inez shared a silent look before she picked up her cell. Her insides shook like Jell-O as she looked at the screen. "It's from Jon," she told Inez. "A police officer will be here in a few minutes."

The officer arrived a moment later. He asked her a lot of questions and then asked for her phone. "And you didn't see anyone suspicious?" he asked after reading the message.

The image of the man she'd run into materialized in her mind. There wasn't a point in telling Officer Denning about her Navy rescuer. She didn't have a name, nor could he offer any more helpful information. "No, sir," she answered. "I didn't see anyone."

After promising to have an officer keep watch over the house until Jon arrived, he gave her his card with his contact info and left them alone.

It took four days for Jon to get an appointment with the man his colleague had recommended. Sutton Smith was a wealthy British man who had a team of security agents that were the best in the business. Weslee still hated the idea of having a bodyguard. She wanted to feel normal again and having someone watching over her wasn't normal. Since the stalker hadn't tried contacting Weslee again, she'd tried several times to talk Jon out of hiring a bodyguard. He wouldn't budge, but their appointment wasn't for a few more hours so she decided to give it one more try.

"Knock-knock," she said, standing in the doorway of the

small den her father used to use when they vacationed here. "I brought you some iced tea and cookies."

Jon looked up from his computer and smiled. "Thank you, sweetheart." He took off his reading glasses and cleared a spot in front of him. "These are my favorite," he said after Weslee deposited the tea and plate of cookies on the desk.

"I know." She smiled and took a seat across from the desk. "I asked Inez to make them just for you."

Eyeing her suspiciously, he ignored the tea and cookies and sat back in his chair. "The answer is no, Weslee."

"Uncle Jon, I don't need a bodyguard." She hoped calling him uncle would soften him up. "My overzealous fan hasn't tried hurting me, nor has he tried contacting me again."

"Stop calling him a fan." Jon pressed his lips together. "He's a stalker, Weslee."

"But he hasn't tried hurting me."

"Well, I'm certainly not going to wait until he does!" He pushed back from the desk and stood up. "Your mother and father asked me to look after you. I can't be with you all the time, and I don't want you alone until we can identify whoever is doing this."

She'd pushed too hard. Jon rarely lost his temper with her. "I'm sorry." She licked her lips. "I didn't mean to upset you."

"Sweetheart, the reason I'm upset is because I love you." He sat on the edge of the desk. "I didn't want to tell you this, but they found the body of one of the missing girls from Duke this morning."

"Oh, that's terrible." Weslee felt sick inside. She knew the girl had been receiving notes from a stalker before she went missing a few weeks earlier. The detective didn't think her stalker was the same person since all of his messages to Weslee were done electronically. "Did they catch the man who did it?"

"No." He looked at her with earnest. "I know Detective

O'Brien doesn't think your case is related, but I'm not willing to take that risk."

"I understand."

"Please don't argue with me further, Weslee." He sighed and ran a hand through his hair. "I'm very close to cancelling your upcoming obligations."

"Please don't cancel my meeting with Mr. Williams," she said, feeling panicked all over again. Company sales had been down slightly this past quarter. If she ever hoped to fill her father's shoes as CEO, she needed to follow through with the marketing ideas she and her team had come up with. Ground Zero had a strong presence on the East Coast. She wanted to do the same out west. If she could get their products in the upscale Total Works Gym and Spa chain headquartered here in San Diego, then she knew she could turn sales around. Especially with all the new products they had coming down the line. "I'm fine having a bodyguard with me," she said, relieved when her uncle nodded his head.

Although she appreciated Jon's concern, sometimes she still felt like a little girl, unable to make big decisions. Part of her wondered if she was ready to hang up her bow and arrow and work behind a desk at Ground Zero. Winning archery tournaments and acting as a spokeswoman for the company had always been her role.

Her notoriety as an archery champion had grown over the past few years, and she'd become the face for Ground Zero and somewhat of a celebrity in the hunting and outdoor industry. Sponsored by her daddy's supplement company, she'd made special appearances at archery tournaments, outdoor sportsman shows, and grand openings for sporting goods stores that carried Ground Zero products.

While she still had several appearances and tournaments scheduled for this year, Weslee knew this would be the last year. The marketing team was already searching for a new face for Ground Zero so she could take over the job as CEO the following year. She had to admit there was a part of her that was eager for the transition. Of course, she wanted to do it in honor of her daddy, but she also wanted to show Dax Hamilton she could be successful without him by her side.

Her former fiancé had left her when she'd needed him most. Right after her parents' funeral. Dax hadn't left her for another girlfriend, but for money. Outdoor Energy, a direct competitor with Ground Zero, had offered Dax an insane amount of money to take over their marketing department. But that wasn't all the company had wanted from him. They wanted insider information. Dax had willingly shared future ideas with his new employer. Ideas that she and Dax had come up with together, including new flavors for the protein powder and the cardio enhancer and recovery drinks. Fortunately, Ground Zero was ahead of schedule and had released the birthday cake flavored protein two weeks before Outdoor Energy introduced a cake batter flavor.

Weslee knew it was only a matter of time before Outdoor Energy got wind of what she was trying to do by getting products into the prestigious gym and spa franchise. Dax would try to infiltrate the same market, using whatever methods he felt were necessary to outbid Ground Zero. She didn't know how he did it, but once this whole stalker thing was taken care of she intended to find out.

Hours later, Weslee and Jon arrived at Sutton Smith's estate. The San Diego cliff-side mansion was breathtaking. Landscaped with lush green lawns and ornate flower gardens, the property reminded her of the famed Biltmore Estate located in Asheville. She'd visited the North Carolina mansion a few times over the years and had come away impressed by the grandeur every time.

Weslee wished she had time to explore the grounds before going inside, but Jon was on a mission and hurried her along by taking her elbow to propel her forward. Even the walkway to the front entrance was impressive, making her wonder how a former officer in the British Armed Forces could afford this estate. She supposed it didn't matter how the man had amassed his fortune. Jon had told her that Mr. Smith used his resources to help others. Weslee's daddy, Marcus, had been the same way. That's why coming to the charity ball had been so important. Weslee was ready to carry on her parents' legacy.

Mr. Smith greeted them personally at the door. Weslee liked his crisp British accent as he invited them into his home. "Pleasure to meet you both," he said, shaking Weslee's hand first.

"Thank you for seeing us, Mr. Smith," Jon said as they shook hands. "My colleague tells me you and your staff are the best in the security business."

"Please call me Sutton." He slipped his hands into his pockets. "And I do believe I have the best security agents," he said in a matter-of-fact way that didn't sound like boasting. "My men and women are vetted thoroughly before I bring them on. Although, the United States Navy does a bang-up job of vetting them first. Most of those working for me have served in the military, and I have a specialized group made up of former SEALs."

Weslee immediately thought about the mysterious naval officer she'd run into the week before. If her bodyguard looked anything like him then this might not be so bad after all.

Sutton led them into an opulent conference room that looked more like something you'd find in Windsor Castle. A man sat at the table, working on his computer. At first glance, Weslee thought the man was the guy from the beach. However, while he was just as handsome and had equally impressive muscles, he was not her Navy rescuer.

He got to his feet and gathered his laptop. "Sorry, sir," he said to Sutton, "I needed a quiet place to do research."

"No worries, mate," Sutton said. "Perhaps you can help me locate Lieutenant Steele? He hasn't responded to the message I sent him earlier."

"Yeah, I'll shoot him a text. I know he went climbing this morning, but he should be home by now." He looked at Weslee and Jon. "Hello."

"Excuse me for not introducing you," Sutton said. "Jace Burns, this is Miss Weslee Campbell and her guardian, Jon Curtis."

"It's nice to meet you, ma'am," he said shaking her hand. "I'm a big fan of you and Ground Zero products."

"Thank you," Weslee said, wishing she could poll him about how he knew her and how he'd been introduced to their supplements. The marketing part of her wanted to know if the targeted ads running on social media were responsible or if someone else had introduced him to their products. "It's nice to meet you too." Weslee offered him a polite smile. While Jace appeared completely competent and would certainly look good in a tux come Saturday, she didn't feel an immediate connection with him. Not that it mattered. She wasn't here to make a connection. She was here to hire someone to protect her.

After Jace shook Jon's hand, Sutton asked him to remain in the room while he tried to find Lieutenant Steele. Agatha, Mr. Smith's housekeeper, served them coffee, and ice water for Weslee. Once she left the room, Jon explained why they were there. Thirty minutes into the meeting, the phone sitting in front of Jace buzzed to life. He glanced at the screen and then pushed his chair back. "Logan's here, sir," he said, getting to his feet.

"Very good," Sutton said. "Take a few minutes to brief him on what we've discussed and then send him in, please."

"Yes, sir," Jace said. He paused and looked at Weslee and smiled. "Ma'am, I'd be honored to protect you, but you'll be in very good hands with Logan. He's had my back since we were kids and he's the best."

"Thank you," she said, hoping Jace's friend was as friendly as he was.

While Sutton and Jon talked logistics about the charity ball the following evening, Weslee kept her eye on the door to the conference room. Nerves tied her stomach into a thousand knots and she tapped her foot to help get rid of the pent-up energy. What did this Logan guy look like? What if he was the huge, sunglass-wearing kind of bodyguard? After hearing the detailed plan, she knew the man would literally be with her all the time, other than private moments in the bathroom and at night. Definitely overkill, but she didn't want to upset Jon again.

A knock sounded at the door. "Come in," Sutton said, turning toward the entrance.

Wesley twisted her hands together as the door opened and in walked exactly what she had feared: a man, sporting huge muscles and wearing sunglasses. *This is never going to work. Why oh why did this have to happen to her?* A pang of disappointment shot through her until he removed the aviators and a familiar pair of blue eyes collided with hers. *Maybe this won't be so bad after all…*

CHAPTER 2

*L*ogan Steele arrived at Sutton's estate, still not sure why his boss wanted him for this protection job. Some of the other men were available. Plus, he was still recovering from his previous assignment that had ended less than a week ago.

Babysitting a spoiled nineteen-year-old girl while protecting her from her crazy ex-boyfriend wasn't exactly what Logan had envisioned when he'd joined Sutton's security firm. Summer Bauer, the daughter of a prominent family in San Diego, had tested him sorely with her relentless flirting and salacious overtures. Heck, the girl made hell week during BUD/S seem like an average PT training session.

Just thinking about his service in the Navy sent his thoughts reeling. Not for the first time, he wondered if he'd made the right decision to retire from the teams. Civilian life wasn't what he'd thought it would be. He felt like something was missing but didn't know what it was. While he enjoyed the success of his cybersecurity company, he missed being a SEAL. That's one of the main reasons he also worked for Sutton. He liked helping people; liked the rush of adrenaline that came with the job. But that empty feeling inside his chest always came back, making him crave his next adventure.

Before cutting the engine to his Jeep, Logan sent a text to Jace telling him he was here. Climbing out of his vehicle, he made his way to the front door of the mansion. The grandeur of the entire property still blew him away. Coming from such a humble home in Colorado left him feeling a little uncomfortable amidst all this money.

He didn't like wealthy people. Actually, that wasn't true. He just disliked rich people that thought they could do whatever they wanted because they have money. Greed, power, and money fueled the evil in this world. It's what had killed Logan's father when he'd died trying to take down a drug lord in South America. And it's what made Logan want to be a SEAL.

Fortunately, Sutton and his wife, Elizabeth, were likable. They weren't anything close to Summer or her parents.

Logan had almost made it to the veranda when Jace came out of the mansion to greet him. "What took you so long?" he asked, glancing at his watch. "I texted you thirty minutes ago."

"Shut up," Logan said, running a hand through his freshly cut hair. Jace knew exactly where he'd been. His team teased him about his standing barber appointment every three weeks. They thought it was due to vanity. He wasn't vain. Just practical. His dark hair was thick and had more than one cowlick. Keeping it trimmed made it easier to deal with. "I had an appointment I couldn't miss."

Jace looked down at his phone and grimaced. "Speaking of appointments, I need to brief you so I'm not late for mine."

"This better not be another teenage-girl babysitting assignment," Logan said. "In fact, why can't I get some dude who likes to watch sports?"

Jace's mouth twitched at the corner. "It doesn't involve a teenage girl." He held up his hand. "And before you even ask, the client is an archery champion named Weslee Campbell."

Wesley Campbell? The guy's name didn't sound familiar, but Logan wasn't into archery either. "Never heard of him."

"You've never heard of *him?*" Jace asked with a laugh.

"Have you?"

"Yeah, man." A smirk settled around Jace's mouth. "Not sure what rock you've been hiding under, but you must be the only guy who doesn't know who Weslee Campbell is."

"What's so special about him?" Logan asked, pulling his phone from his pocket. "Maybe I should look him up."

"No time. Sutton is waiting for you," Jace said, jerking his thumb over his shoulder to point to the house. "All you need to know is Weslee has a stalker and needs twenty-four-hour protection until the authorities find out who is sending the messages."

"What is it with all these stalkers?" Logan immediately thought about the pretty girl on the beach. He had mixed emotions about how he'd handled the whole thing. He should've insisted they call the police right then. He'd been so concerned about her safety that he'd jogged by the house early the next morning and later in the evening, hoping to run into her again. Not literally—he'd already done that—but he regretted not getting her name or phone number.

He told himself he only wanted her contact info so he could make sure she was okay, not because he wanted to hear her soft southern drawl and offer to take her to dinner.

"We live in a crazy world," Jace said, edging past him. "Wish I could stick around, but I've gotta go."

"Hey," Logan called out, "Are you up for climbing this weekend?"

"Don't think you'll have time," Jace said without breaking

his stride. "But let me know what you think of Weslee Campbell."

Knowing he better not keep Sutton waiting any longer, Logan entered the house and hurried to the conference room. The door was closed, so he knocked once and then pushed the door open when Sutton called for him to come inside.

Logan's lungs seized the second he entered the room. It was her. The same beautiful girl he'd been trying to forget ever since running into her a few nights earlier. His military training had taught him to keep his emotions neutral. Still, he kept his sunglasses on long enough to check his reaction before he took them off and met her startled gaze.

Was *she* the archery champion? His eyes flickered to the man sitting next to her. Or was *he*?

"Logan," Sutton said, snapping him from his musings. "I'd like to introduce you to Weslee Campbell."

Keeping his focus away from the pretty girl, he crossed the room and held out his hand to the man. "It's nice to meet you, sir."

"Pardon me?" the man said with a lift of an eyebrow.

Heat pooled in his gut as Logan dropped his hand to his side and shifted his attention to the pretty blonde.

"Apparently, you're not a fan, but I'm Weslee Campbell," the woman said, amusement lighting her aquamarine colored eyes. "Don't worry about it. It happens all the time. I was named after my daddy but my mother insisted on spelling it differently."

He was going to kill Jace. The guy knew all along the client was a *her* not a him.

"Sorry, ma'am," Logan said, holding out his hand. "Logan Steele."

Her perfectly shaped lips curved up as she placed her palm against his. He wasn't prepared for the powerful zing of heat that burned through him. He wanted to jerk back and put some distance between them, but he held perfectly still.

Her smile wavered as she glanced down at their hands. "I think we've met before," she said, quickly withdrawing her hand. "Unless you don't remember me?"

Logan held back a sarcastic laugh. He remembered her all too well. "Yes, ma'am, we've met before." He kept how often he'd tried to forget her the past few days to himself. "Did you ever contact the police?"

"Weslee, when did you meet him?" her companion asked, clearly not pleased with her. "And why didn't you tell me about him?"

The irritation in his voice rubbed Logan the wrong way. Was the guy her father? Surely not her boyfriend. "We ran into each other on the beach the other night. She was upset because of a text message from a guy she didn't know."

"You knew about her stalker and didn't do anything about it?" the man asked, his eyes flashing with anger. He turned to look at Sutton. "I don't think this is going to work."

"I disagree, Jon," Sutton said. "Logan's skills are exactly the kind needed to provide Miss Campbell with the best protection."

"Uncle Jon," Weslee said, her soft southern drawl cajoling the man's anger away from Logan. "I'm the one who quite literally ran into Mr. Steele." She moistened her lips and glanced quickly at Logan. "He did help me by searching the area thoroughly for an intruder. He also offered to call the police, but I refused and then hurried back to the house to help Inez."

Logan appreciated her defense of him. He appreciated a lot of things about her. How could this beautiful woman, who looked more like a super-model, be an archery champion? His gaze traveled over her delicate features, noting her flawless, golden skin didn't have one freckle that usually came from being in the sun. Her long hair was like spun gold, shimmering under the chandelier's lights. Somehow, he knew her hair was soft and would smell just as good.

Jace was right about one thing...what rock *had* he been living under to not know about this girl?

Logan looked at Weslee's uncle just in time to see a smile soften his mouth. "I apologize, young man. I'm Jon Curtis."

"No apologies necessary, sir," Logan said, grasping the man's hand. "I'm assuming the police couldn't find anything since you both are here?"

"That's right." Grave lines creased the man's forehead. "While this man has never outright threatened Weslee, I'm concerned about the tone of his messages."

Logan took a seat next to Sutton and asked for further details. The stalker usually messaged her on social media. They still weren't clear how he'd gotten her cell phone number. Logan could figure that one out with the right equipment and some time.

"I've printed out all of the previous messages," Jon said, sliding a folder over to Logan. "You can read for yourself that he's focused on Weslee's appearance."

Logan opened the folder, noting the spelling of her name as he read over some of the messages. He didn't like the tone either. Clearly, the guy was a little unhinged. He was obsessed with Weslee, particularly her hair. Logan chastised himself for his earlier desire to feel how soft her hair was. Her stalker mentioned her hair in each message, fantasizing about touching it or running his fingers through it.

He directed most of his questions to Jon, whom he'd discovered wasn't really related to Weslee. He was her father's closest friend and the attorney for Ground Zero.

Ground Zero, the nutritional supplement company her

father had created, he had heard of. The company focused on the outdoor sports community rather than just the traditional athlete. Some of the guys at the gym he frequented used the company's products religiously. Now that he thought about it, he had seen Weslee's picture before. Only instead of wearing the gray dress slacks and pale pink blouse she had on today, she'd dressed in full camouflage, a Ground Zero ball cap, and held her bow.

Every time he or Sutton asked Weslee a direct question, Logan told himself that her southern accent wasn't anything special. He'd heard it hundreds of times over the years. He also ignored the pull of attraction he felt each time she spoke or their eyes met. He was a professional and wouldn't let his feelings get in the way of protecting her.

Besides, she couldn't be more than twenty—totally off limits. He sure hoped this wealthy barely-not-a-teenage-girl wasn't anything like Summer. Unlike his last security detail where they knew the identity of the stalker, Weslee's stalker was an unknown. Logan's job protecting her could go on for months. If Weslee tried any of the seduction tactics Summer had used on him, he wasn't entirely sure he could resist her.

The thought made him feel weak. Logan wasn't weak. He was a former SEAL, trained to withstand brutal circumstances. He had survived three months in a Syrian prison the previous year after his SEAL team had been captured, and then escaped with his team by piloting a rickety helicopter without any previous experience. That act could've been labeled as stupid, but he wasn't weak.

Drawing on skills he'd honed as a SEAL, he viewed Weslee as only the mission. He needed to keep her safe, find the threat and then eliminate it.

Jon handed both Logan and Sutton a list of her scheduled appearances over the next month. "Are all of these necessary for you to attend?" Logan asked Weslee, reading over the events. Most of them were held in sporting goods stores or gyms, which would be easier to secure. The outdoor archery tournament scheduled for the first week in April made him uneasy. He'd need backup, preferably from his former SEAL team. Since the event wasn't for another three weeks, he'd have to find out if they were involved with other assignments. Otherwise, he'd utilize off-duty police officers.

"Yes," she said.

"No," Jon said at the same time. Her guardian sighed with frustration. "Weslee, please be reasonable. Do you really have to attend every single event?"

"I thought that was the whole reason for a bodyguard." She looked directly at Logan. "Are you saying you can't protect me?"

"No, ma'am." He narrowed his eyes, not liking the insinuation that he wasn't competent. She didn't back down under his glare, which equally irritated him and impressed him. "I'm simply asking a question."

"Oh." She clasped her hands together in front of her. "I suppose I can forfeit some of the appearances, but I don't want to miss the tournament. It's a charitable event to raise money for leukemia research."

"Okay." Logan glanced down at the paper and back up again. "It's in North Carolina?"

"Yes, and it's important to me to be there. One of my best friends died from leukemia our senior year in high school. Her mother had raised her and her little brother on her own and wanted to do something to remember her and help at the same time. My parents organized Melanie's Find the Cure tournament a few years back, and Janice, Melanie's mother, has run it ever since." Weslee's eyes shimmered with moisture. "I couldn't attend last year due to scheduling conflicts, but

Janice called me a few months ago and asked if I could be there."

"All right." Logan glanced at Sutton. "The tournament isn't for another three weeks so we've got some time to work out all the logistics."

"Excellent," Sutton said with a nod of his head. "What are your thoughts about the event tomorrow evening?"

"What event?" Logan asked.

Weslee answered, explaining about the charity event held annually at the Hotel del Coronado that benefitted children and needy families.

"In conjunction with the fundraiser," Weslee continued, "Ground Zero donates all the proceeds for the entire month of March to help feed kids who are starving right in our own backyards." She lifted her chin a notch. "Mama and Daddy haven't missed it once since they started attending ten years ago, and I won't miss it either."

While Logan appreciated her desire to help children, the timeframe to prep for the event was limited. He'd only been to the historic hotel once so he wasn't familiar enough with the structure to ensure her safety. Before Logan could shoot it down, Sutton gave his approval.

"Given the location and the high-priced ticket cost for each guest, I don't see why you can't attend, Miss Campbell." Sutton turned to Logan. "Are you okay with that?"

"I suppose I don't have a choice," Logan said, crossing his arms over his chest. "Am I right?" he asked Weslee.

"I'm not trying to be difficult, Mr. Steele." Frustration flashed in her light blue eyes. "It's one of the main reasons I'm here, but I'm sure we can make other arrangements if you don't wish to attend."

She was going to be difficult in every way. Difficult to

control and difficult not to like. "Since I *am* going with you I think you can call me Logan, ma'am."

A small smile edged up one side of her mouth. "All right, Logan." Her lips parted to reveal perfect, white teeth. "But will you stop addressing me as ma'am? It makes me feel older than twenty-five."

She was twenty-five? That meant she was only four years younger than him. He narrowed his eyes, feeling annoyed that she wasn't as off-limits as he'd thought. "We'll stay for the auction, ma'am...I mean, Weslee."

The sweet smile slipped. "But what about the dance?"

"What about it?" He was not going to spend the entire evening watching her dance with other men. That was a security nightmare. If he dug deep enough he knew he'd find another reason why watching her dance with other men wasn't acceptable.

He wasn't digging.

"I understand if you aren't comfortable dancing." She offered him another smile. "I certainly don't expect you to dance with me."

Logan wasn't uncomfortable dancing. His mother had made him take a dance class right before he joined the ROTC in high school, telling him that every naval officer needed to know how to dance for the Navy Ball. So, yeah, he could dance. He just wasn't sure he wanted to dance with her.

"Logan is an excellent dancer," Sutton said, clapping Logan on the shoulder. "I'll make sure my tailor fits him for a tux this evening."

A *tux*? Why did rich people like to dress in the most uncomfortable clothes known to man? Wearing a tux meant wearing a tie. He hated wearing ties.

"How wonderful," Weslee said, sounding anything but happy. Clearly, she didn't want Logan as her date any more than he wanted to be there. She reached for her glass of water and took a sip, keeping her gaze averted from him. When she set the glass down, she accidentally knocked it over. "Oh my goodness," she said, jumping up from her chair. "I'm so sorry."

"No worries, dear girl," Sutton said, handing her a napkin. "It's just water."

She pulled at the fabric of her pink blouse, which had become slightly transparent. It didn't reveal anything but she asked to be excused to the restroom. Sutton told her the location of the bathroom, offering to have Agatha bring her dry clothing.

"No, thank you," she said. "I'll only be a moment."

Once she was gone, Jon leaned forward, looking directly at Logan. "The ball is important to Weslee, but I'm worried about her safety." He glanced over his shoulder. "Just this morning, the North Carolina police found the body of one of the missing college students from Duke. They don't have a suspect in custody but believe it's a man who's been stalking her for the past few months."

"The same stalker?" Logan asked, wondering why they were even talking about allowing Weslee to attend any public events with a murderer out there.

"No. At least the police tell me it's not related." He explained how her stalker's MO was not the same. The girl from Duke had received only handwritten notes whereas Weslee's stalker has used digital means like social media, email or her cell phone. Although they'd recently changed Weslee's phone number, the guy had managed to find it again. "Aside from the different methods used, the stalkers for both girls started in the same time frame, about six weeks ago. The detective said it was unlikely a stalker would pursue two women at the same time."

"Does Miss Campbell know about the other girl?" Sutton asked.

"I told her this morning." His forehead creased with worry lines. "It's the only way I could convince her to agree to have a bodyguard."

Logan drummed his fingers on the table, considering everything he'd just been told. The auction was risky, but not as risky as the dance afterward. Men would be asking Weslee to the dance floor. Men she most likely didn't know. How could he guarantee her stalker wasn't among the elite patrons? Or he could pose as a staff member to get inside the doors. Both Jon and Sutton agreed with him when he voiced his concerns.

"You could pose as her date," Jon suggested.

"Yes," Logan said, "but I've been to a few formal dances with a date and it didn't stop other men from asking her to dance."

"That won't be a problem if her date is a possessive boyfriend," Sutton said with a small smirk. "You have years of covert operation experience, Lieutenant Steele. However, I doubt any of those ops were as pleasant as this one."

Logan shifted on his seat, keeping his expression as neutral as possible. He wasn't worried about roleplaying Weslee Campbell's possessive boyfriend. What worried him more was how much he liked the idea of being her boyfriend. There was something about her that got to him. She'd been on his mind ever since running into her on the beach. If he didn't watch himself, he'd be as whooped as Blaine Hammerton. His former SEAL teammate was now a married man.

Weslee Campbell was the mission. Logan needed to remember that.

"I'm trusting you to take care of her," Jon said, his voice wobbly with emotion. "She's like a daughter to me, and I don't want anything to happen to her."

"Yes, sir," Logan said, reaffirming in his mind that she was the mission. "I will guard her with my life."

They discussed the merits of staying in the main house in North Carolina or the family's beach house once they left San Diego. Both homes had sophisticated security systems already in place. Her home outside of Raleigh was larger and had more unfavorable variables, such as the heavily wooded area in the back, so they all agreed the beach house on Emerald Isle was the best place to keep her safe. The private beach had security guards at both entrances, limiting the access to the house.

Jon asked that they not say anything about staying at the beach house until after the charity ball. Weslee hadn't been back there since her parents had died, and Mr. Curtis didn't want to upset her. "She's already not going to like having you assigned as her boyfriend."

Logan was okay with that. Things would be a lot more complicated if she wanted him for a boyfriend. He wasn't good boyfriend material anyway. It wasn't that he couldn't commit or be faithful. He wasn't a player, and he didn't mess around with women for pleasure. The problem was a sense that he wasn't good enough for someone like Weslee. She was so innocent and untainted with a giving heart. He was cynical, had witnessed a lot of crap and done things he still had nightmares about.

Weslee came back into the room, the front of her shirt nearly dry. Taking her seat, Jon gave her an update, and he was right...she did not like the idea of Logan posing as her boyfriend.

"Honestly, Jon, I don't understand why this is necessary." She spared Logan a quick glance before continuing on with her impassioned speech. "Mr. Steele will be right there watching me dance. And it's not likely any of the men asking to dance with me will be my stalker. Even if he is there, he isn't going to do anything to me with Mr. Steele present and in a room full of people."

Mr. Steele? What happened to using first names? And why was she making such a big deal out of it and talking like he wasn't in the room? His male ego didn't like her vehement response. It was one thing for him to admit he wasn't good boyfriend material…quite another for someone who didn't know jack about him to make that call.

"Weslee, please don't be difficult." Jon rubbed his head. "I feel a migraine coming on and I don't want to argue about this further."

Logan kept his mouth shut. Frankly, it was probably a good idea if Sutton assigned another protection agent to watch over her. The fact that he even remotely cared about her response was a red flag.

"All right, I won't argue," she said, looking at her uncle. "And I'm sorry your head hurts."

"This is for your good, sweetheart."

"I know." She looked at Sutton. "I apologize for my rude behavior. It's just been a stressful day."

"No need to apologize," Sutton said, his chipper British accent as pleasant as ever. "I understand how high emotions ride with this type of situation."

Logan waited for her to address him. Apparently, he didn't warrant an apology. Without meeting his eyes, she pushed back from the table and stood up. "Thank you for taking the job, Mr. Steele. I appreciate your willingness to watch out for me until the police find out who is sending me the messages."

"Just doing my job, ma'am," he said, getting to his feet. If she noticed he didn't use her first name, she didn't show it. In fact, she never made eye contact with him again, not even when she said goodbye.

At Jon's request, Sutton sent an escort from his regular staff of security agents, giving Logan a chance to go home and pack. They would leave for North Carolina on a private jet right after the ball, which eliminated him worrying about keeping her safe at the airport.

He texted Jace once he was in his Jeep. *Thanks for the heads-up, pal. I made a fool out of myself when I addressed her guardian as Mr. Campbell.*

Jace called him back instead of texting him. He was laughing too hard to speak so Logan hung up on him. He headed for home, ignoring Jace's attempts to call him back. His friend was waiting for him at his condo when he pulled in ten minutes later.

"Shut up," Logan said when Jace cracked up again. He unlocked the front door and pushed it open.

"Sorry." Jace followed him inside before he could lock him out. "I'm done laughing."

"Right." Logan headed for the kitchen to get a drink of water. "Don't you have somewhere else to be?" he asked. "I thought you had an appointment?"

"I did. With In-N-Out." He sat down on one of the barstools. "Wish I had your assignment, but Sutton made it pretty clear he only wanted you for the job."

"Of course he wanted me." Logan opened his fridge, frowning at how empty it was. "I'm the best op he has." He grabbed a bottle of water and closed the fridge.

"You think that's why he picked you?" Jace asked with a snort. "Dude, take a look at Sutton's other men. He handpicked them for each assignment and they all ended up engaged or married."

"Sutton isn't into matchmaking. He just needs my computer skills." He unscrewed the cap and took a drink of water. "Even if that were true, I'm not getting married to Weslee Campbell. She's the mission. End of story."

"So you don't think she's hot?" Jace asked.

"She's pretty, but I'm not interested," he said, taking a long drink, nearly emptying the bottle.

"Dude, you need to get that mystery girl out of your system. You'll never see her again."

Logan choked on the water, spewing the contents in his mouth across the countertop and onto the front of Jace's shirt. In a moment of weakness, he'd told Jace all about his encounter with the pretty blonde he'd run into. Jace was the one who had encouraged him to go back to the same stretch of beach to look for her, suggesting he just knock on the door. Not wanting to come off as another stalker, Logan had never approached the house. Besides, the house had appeared unoccupied. He figured the pretty girl had gone back home to wherever she was from.

"Was it something I said?" Jace asked, standing up and pulling the wet fabric away from his body.

Logan ignored his friend's question. There was no way he'd ever tell him that Weslee was the mystery woman. Grabbing a wad of paper towels, he threw it at Jace and then tore off another section to wipe down the counter.

"Wait a minute," Jace said, eyeing him with suspicion. "You saw that girl again, didn't you?"

"I saw her." Logan had learned a long time ago it was better to stick closer to the truth when withholding information. "It was no big deal. Besides, she was with another guy."

"That bites."

"Yeah, but she wasn't as pretty as I remembered." Logan shrugged and tossed his water bottle in the recycling bin. He wasn't lying. Weslee was much prettier than he'd remembered.

Before Jace asked more questions, Logan briefed him on the plans to keep Weslee safe.

"You dog," Jace said when he heard Logan was flying on a

private jet to a secluded beach house in North Carolina. "Are you sure you don't need backup?"

"I might, but I'm not calling you if I do." He headed out of the kitchen to go pack his bags. "Not after you let me make a fool out of myself."

"Oh come on. That was funny," Jace said. "Seriously, how could you not know Weslee Campbell is the hot girl from Ground Zero?"

"Because I use the stuff from Outdoor Energy."

"Better not let Weslee hear you say that," Jace said from behind him. "They're rival companies."

"Guess I can't pack any of my Outdoor Energy shirts then."

That made Jace laugh. "Since she's just *the mission*, I'd pack a few of them just in case she makes the moves on you." He grinned when Logan shot him a surly look. "For whatever reason, wealthy, beautiful women find you attractive."

"Summer Bauer was not a woman."

One of Jace's brows lifted. "Dude, I saw her. She is definitely a woman."

"She's nineteen."

"Eighteen is considered an adult."

"Why don't you remind her she's an adult the next time she pitches a fit for her daddy to buy her a Tesla even though she's driving a new Mercedes Crossover."

"At least she has good taste in cars." Jace slugged Logan in the arm. "Her taste in men is highly questionable."

Logan smirked and threw a wadded-up Outdoor Energy shirt at him. "North Carolina is sounding better and better."

Thankfully Jace had a date and left Logan alone to finish packing. He wasn't sure how long the job would last, but he packed for two weeks. If the op went on longer than that, he knew how to do laundry.

The drive didn't take long. Logan frequently ran this

stretch of beach, so he was familiar with the ritzy homes. But as he parked his Jeep in front of the bungalow, he felt like he was about to face enemy insurgents. He took in the opulent dwelling and shook his head. His idea of a bungalow was not congruent with the gorgeous ocean-front house. He knew what property cost in San Diego and this was a prime location. It was hard to imagine the house was only used a few times a year.

Climbing out of his Jeep, he took note of his surroundings. If stalker-fan-boy knew Weslee was staying here then he was probably watching right now. Logan didn't catch sight of any lurking strangers as he approached the front door.

The security agent from Sutton's opened the door for him. The scent of freshly baked bread made Logan's mouth water, reminding him that he'd missed dinner.

"Everything quiet?" he asked the man.

"Yes, sir." The guy glanced at his watch. "Jenkins will be here at 2300. You can call me if anything comes up before then."

"Thanks, man," Logan said, shaking his hand. He waited for the guard to exit before he closed the door and locked it. Eager to check out what smelled so good, Logan turned and almost plowed over Weslee. "Hey," he said, unable to hide his smile when her eyes zeroed in on his shirt.

Self-preservation and a little streak of rebellion made Logan wear one of his Outdoor Energy shirts. Weslee Campbell was not happy about it.

CHAPTER 3

*W*eslee wasn't prone to violence, but after the message from Dax, her traitorous ex-fiancé, she wanted to take a pair of scissors to Logan's shirt. Given the smug look on his handsome face, she knew that's exactly the reaction he wanted. She eyed the shirt's design concept and almost demanded that he take it off right now. However, seeing the former SEAL shirtless wouldn't help her cause in trying not to be attracted to him.

"Hello, Mr. Steele."

"Mr. Steele?" he said, quirking a dark eyebrow. "You remember my name's Logan, right?"

"Forgive me," she said, giving him a tight smile. "It somehow slipped my mind."

"No worries." He pointed to her Ground Zero shirt. "Nice shirt."

"Thank you." She narrowed her gaze. "Wish I could say the same about yours."

A wicked grin split his face before he laughed outright. Weslee tried not to notice the dimple in his cheek, but there it was, making his chiseled face boyishly charming. She ordered her body to stop reacting to this man. The butterflies dancing in her stomach completely ignored her demands.

"Do you want me to take the shirt off?" His fingers tugged at the hem, lifting the edge just enough to give her a small preview of sculpted abs.

Yes! the butterflies said as they fluttered wildly in her stomach. "Absolutely not!" she said, reaching out to pull the shirt back down. Her fingers grazed the hard wall of his muscled stomach, and she froze. He did too.

Barely able to draw in her next breath, she looked up at him. Blue eyes the color of sapphires held her captive. The amusement faded away as something undefinable flickered in its place.

"Weslee?" Inez called out from the kitchen. Weslee jumped back from Logan just as Inez entered the room. "Oh, hello, Mr. Steele." She wiped her hands on the front of her apron. "I'm Inez Markham."

"Logan Steele," he said, taking Inez's small hand in his. "It's nice to meet you, ma'am."

"Likewise." The friendly smile disappeared from her nanny's face as she glared at Logan's shirt. "We have a dress code here, young man," she said, snapping both her hands to her thick waist. "And it doesn't include that T-shirt."

A wry grin lifted the corner of his mouth. "Yes, ma'am. Miss Campbell already informed me of that." A playful gleam danced in his eyes. "She almost ripped it right off me."

"I did not," Weslee said. "I'm the one who kept your shirt on."

"Why on earth would you do that?" Inez asked, like taking off a former Navy SEAL's shirt was completely normal. "Take it off him, and I'll burn it for good measure."

Logan watched her closely, probably thinking she was

crazy. The only thing crazy was that she'd ever considered marrying Dax in the first place. When her ex had jumped ship and started working for Outdoor Energy, he'd stolen Weslee's design concept for the very shirt Logan was wearing.

"I'm sorry about the shirt," Logan said. "I promise never to wear it again in your presence."

"If you want any of my biscuits and gravy you will never wear it again. Period." Inez held out her hand, palm up. "Hand it over."

"Inez!" Weslee said. "He doesn't need to take off his shirt right now." She shot Logan an irritated look. "He can wait until he's in his room."

"New shirt, young man," Inez said, shaking a finger at him. "Or no supper for you."

Logan laughed and held up his hands in surrender. "I'm sorry, ma'am. I'll go dispose of it right now."

"Thank you."

Weslee waited until Inez went back into the kitchen before she dared look at Logan. She was embarrassed by her poor manners. "I'm sorry for overreacting. It's been a bad...let's just say that on any other night I would've laughed it off."

"Something tells me Ms. Markham would still feel the same way."

"She's just very overprotective of me."

He studied her, his dark lashes hiding his eyes. "I'm guessing there's a story behind this shirt?"

"Yes, but now it seems silly that I reacted that way." She bit her bottom lip. "I'm truly sorry. You're welcome to wear...keep the shirt...I still wouldn't advise you wear it if you want to eat any of Inez's cooking."

He laughed softly. "I'll go change just as soon as you point out my room."

Weslee showed him his room, which was situated on the

main floor. The view from this room was stunning. French doors opened onto a balcony overlooking the ocean. Her parents had always stayed in this room whenever they visited. Weslee could picture her mama sitting on one of the chairs reading while her daddy sat across from her working on his laptop. "I hope this will be okay," she said, stepping aside to give Logan a clear path into the room.

He eased past her, and she caught the masculine scent of his soap. It smelled better than the key lime pie Inez had made for dessert. "This room is amazing," he said, turning back to look at her. "I didn't kick anyone out of here, did I?"

"No." She crossed her arms as if hugging herself. "My parents used to stay here."

Compassion crossed his features. "I'm sorry," he said. "I'm sure this is hard for you."

Not trusting her voice, Weslee nodded her head. Someday she would stay in this room, perhaps with her future husband. For now, she was happy in the yellow room on the second floor.

"Hey," Logan said, "I'm fine sleeping on the couch."

"That's not necessary." She eyed his large, muscular frame. "My daddy was tall too, so this room has a California King bed. I doubt you'd be comfortable on the couch."

"I've slept in plenty of uncomfortable places before when on assignment." He smiled and placed his duffle bag on the floor. "These are by far the nicest accommodations."

Weslee wanted to ask him about the places he'd been during his time in the Navy. She wanted to ask him about his childhood, his family. Basically, she wanted to get to know him. He seemed to fill up this entire room with his presence. What was it about him that drew her to him? It wasn't just his looks. Maybe it was his desire to protect people. She remembered what he'd said that night on the beach when she'd run into him. *I protect women not hurt them.*

She needed to put any romantic notions aside. Protecting people is what Logan Steele did for a living. His role as her boyfriend was merely that: A role to play.

"Let me know if you need anything," she said before leaving him to get settled.

She was grateful they were only staying one night. Having him here made the house feel small. She would be glad when they were back home. Well, not exactly home. Jon had informed her that the house on Emerald Isle was safer than her parent's mansion. At least with the three-story beach house, Logan could have his own floor to himself. Unless he insisted on staying on the top floor where she and Inez had their rooms.

Weslee had mixed emotions about going to the beach house. It was the last place her parents had been alive. They'd died on the drive home when their car slid off the road and rolled down an embankment. It had been raining that day, but not anything her daddy hadn't driven in before. The police didn't know if her father had swerved to miss an animal, but he'd lost control of the car at the wrong place. If it had happened on any other spot on the road then they would still be alive.

Inez had just pulled out the pan of buttermilk biscuits. The heavenly scent tempted Weslee to snitch one like she'd done so many times over the years. "It smells divine in here," she said, sliding onto one of the bar stools. "I'd offer to help, but we both know I'd end up burning something."

"That's the truth," Inez said with a laugh. "Don't know how you do it, but you do."

Weslee sighed. She'd inherited her mama's blue eyes and

blonde hair, but absolutely none of her cooking skills. "What would I do without you?"

"Starve," Inez said, winking at her. She leaned forward and looked toward the hallway. "Despite his taste in clothing, that man is as delicious as my key lime pie."

"He's my bodyguard."

"A handsome bodyguard posing as your boyfriend." Inez straightened up. "Come to think of it, he looks like that man who helped you last week."

"Um, I forgot to tell you...he is the man who helped me last week." Inez got that look in her eyes as a slow smile spread across her face. Weslee held up a hand to put a stop to any notions her former nanny was conjuring in that brain of hers. "It's a coincidence, Inez. Nothing more."

"I don't believe in coincidences." Her eyes sparkled with delight. "It's divine destiny, honey. I'm sure of it."

"No—" Weslee started to argue, but Logan walked into the kitchen, cutting off her denial.

"Good thing I brought a few other shirts," Logan said. "Because dinner smells delicious."

The meal was good, not that Inez had ever cooked anything inedible. However, Logan appreciated it more than anyone. Proving it by eating a large second helping of everything.

Inez loved it. Jon never had seconds, neither did she. It was obvious her housekeeper liked Logan, but he completely won her over the moment she brought out the key lime pie. "Ma'am, don't tell my mother this but your cooking is the best I've ever tasted."

Inez beamed. "Well, aren't you just the sweetest man." She gave Weslee a pointed look—something she'd done throughout the meal—as if to tell her she'd better lay claim to him before someone else did. Weslee wished Inez would stop.

The former SEAL earned more points with her nanny

when he insisted on cleaning up the table. Inez cast her another meaningful look. Before Inez said anything embarrassing, Weslee scooted back from the table. "Please excuse me, but I need to speak with Jon about a business matter." He'd taken his meal in his office, trying to catch up on work he'd gotten behind on over the past few days.

Without waiting for a response, Weslee hurried out of the kitchen to find Jon. She hadn't exactly lied since there was always something about the business to discuss. Besides, she wanted another chance to convince Jon she didn't need her bodyguard to pose as her boyfriend, or maybe ask Sutton if there was another security agent available that she didn't find quite so attractive. Instant attraction, she'd learned, was a fickle thing. She'd felt that way around Dax, though never to this extent. That's why she needed to steer clear of developing any more feelings for Logan Steele. The best way to do that was to not spend any more time with him.

The door to Jon's office was cracked open, and she heard him talking on his phone about a legal matter with one of their vendors. She frowned, knowing he wouldn't be done with this conversation for at least another hour. The man worked too hard. Even his earlier headache hadn't stopped him from working. Weslee wished he would slow down and find another wife. He'd been a widower for nearly twenty years now. At fifty-nine he was still handsome with only a touch of gray showing in his dark hair.

Tiptoeing away from the office, she ventured toward the sliding glass door that led to the back porch. She tugged on a string to open the blinds, giving her a view of the ocean. The wispy clouds along the horizon promised another stunning sunset was on the way. She longed to walk on the beach, and it frustrated her that she simply couldn't go outside and enjoy the evening.

She felt trapped. Part of her wanted to sneak outside without telling anyone. Her stalker had never threatened her with violence. She doubted he would actually hurt her. Then she thought about the dead girl from Duke University. Had she thought the same thing about her stalker? Weslee had found the story online and read that the girl was last seen walking home from a party. Her apartment was only a couple of blocks away, but somewhere in-between the party and home, she'd vanished.

With Logan and Inez still talking in the kitchen, she carefully slid the door open and drew in a lungful of the salty air. A soft breeze ruffled her hair, beckoning her to step outside. She wouldn't venture far, just stay right here on the deck.

"You're not planning to go out, right?" Logan said from behind her.

Startled, Weslee jumped back and turned to look at him. "Maybe," she said with a tiny bit of attitude. She wasn't normally so prickly but Logan flustered her.

Furrowing his brow, he crossed the floor and slid the door closed. "You shouldn't open any doors without me there, let alone go outside unprotected."

"It's not fair," she said, turning to look out the glass. She'd been a prisoner to her grief and now she was literally a prisoner because of someone's fixation on her.

"I know." His voice held compassion as he moved to stand next to her. "But it is necessary."

She kept her gaze focused on the horizon, trying to ignore the clean scent of his soap. "I feel like Jon has blown this all out of proportion. The guy messaging me hasn't ever threatened me or tried to hurt me."

"Not yet," Logan said, his deep voice serious.

She drew in a sharp breath and looked up at him. "You think he'll hurt me?"

Logan peered down at her. "It's concerning that he followed you here, which means he's unpredictable."

"What if we set up a meeting with him?" A shiver of apprehension slid over her skin like her subconscious recognized how unwise it would be to make contact. "I mean, if he just wants to meet me then maybe he'll stop harassing me."

"Not a good idea," Logan said. "Contacting him would only fuel his obsession. I've read the previous messages, Weslee. The guy has never once requested a meeting." His gaze traveled the length of her long hair that hung over one shoulder. "His focus is on the clothes you're wearing, how they fit your body and your hair. My worry is that he sees you only as an object, not a person. That makes him doubly dangerous."

"I hate this," she said, feeling her lower lip tremble. "My daddy loved taking me for an evening walk along the beach. We'd let the water roll over our feet while we waited for the perfect moment to take a picture of the sunset."

"He was a photographer?" Logan asked.

"An amateur one." She told him all about her daddy's attempts to capture the perfect picture. She glanced up at him to find him looking at her. "I only have one more night here. I don't know when I'll be back in San Diego, so I'd like the chance to try and get the perfect picture for my daddy."

He considered her for a long moment. Then he pulled his cell from his pocket. "Let me make a few calls to see about getting another set of eyes. After eating so much food a walk on the beach sounds good to me too."

"Thank you," Weslee said, surprised by his kindness. She knew her ex-fiancé wouldn't have cared if she had to stay indoors. Logan nodded his head and then walked to the corner of the room to talk on his phone.

Thinking about Dax and the email he'd sent her earlier made her stomach feel like she'd swallowed rocks for supper. Her ex had no business creeping back into her life; no right to say how much he missed her or to ask her to meet with him, so they could talk about what had happened between them and a possible future together.

There was no future. Dax didn't want her back. He just wanted her because she'd inherited a lot of money, as well as her father's shares in Ground Zero.

Truly, it was a blessing Dax had left her when he did. Once they'd broken up, it had become crystal clear how selfish he was while they'd been together. If Outdoor Energy hadn't already put the wheels in motion and given Dax a huge signing bonus before her parent's accident, he would've never left.

Logan ended the call and twenty minutes later escorted her outside. Before leaving, Weslee pulled on a hot-pink hoodie over her shirt. The fitted sweatshirt was a limited edition that featured a lime green embroidered logo of Ground Zero on the upper left side of her chest.

Logan waited for her at the bottom of the steps, scanning their surroundings. He didn't have a jacket on, and the new shirt he'd changed into fit him almost like a second skin. His muscles really were impressive. They weren't huge like some of the steroid-induced, vein-popping muscles she'd seen at the various gyms she'd been to over the years, but they were rock solid and very capable of protecting her.

She noticed that he still wore the thin-corded bracelets and was sliding his thumb along the outside of one of them as he searched the perimeter. Again, she wondered where he'd gotten them. According to Sutton, Logan had never been married. Of course, that didn't mean he hadn't fathered a child.

He dropped his hand and looked up at her as she descended the stairs. Before heading out, she slipped off her shoes and dropped them next to the stairs. "Thank you for doing this," she said, letting her toes sink into the cool sand.

"You're welcome." He moved aside and indicated with his hand for her to start walking. "Lead the way."

She headed for the shoreline, and he followed close beside her. He was quiet, his teasing mood from earlier completely gone. She hoped his reticence wasn't because Inez had filled his head with her romantic ideas that he and Weslee were destined to be together.

They walked in silence for several yards until Weslee couldn't stand it anymore. "Since we're going to be spending a lot of time together, I'd like to know a little bit more about you."

"Like what?" he asked, eyeing her suspiciously.

She sidestepped a clump of seaweed. "Like, where did you grow up or have you always lived in San Diego?"

He didn't answer her right away. It wasn't until Weslee looked at him again that he finally spoke. "I spent most of my childhood in Colorado."

"Only most of it?"

He regarded her with another long look. "My mom and I moved to Colorado after my dad passed away."

"I'm sorry," Weslee said, feeling another connection with him. He knew what it felt like to lose a parent. "How old were you?"

"Ten," he said, staring straight ahead.

Weslee wanted to know more, but his rigid body language suggested he didn't want to talk about it. She got that. It had taken a few months before she could talk about her parent's death. Everyone handled grief differently. Logan had only been a child when his daddy had died, which had to make healing so much harder.

"Goodness," she said with a squeal as the water rushed in and covered her bare feet. "That's cold."

Logan reacted lightning fast, taking her by the hand and pulling her back. The warmth from his touch radiated through her, stealing her breath. She raised her face to look at him, and their eyes connected. She wished she could read minds...she had no idea if Logan felt this pull between them like she did.

"You should've left your shoes on," he said, abruptly dropping her hand.

The gruff tone of his voice left her feeling like she'd been doused over the head with a wave of cold water. If he did feel anything for her, then he hid it well or didn't like it. Either way, it was for the best.

Shoving her hands into the large pocket of her hoodie, she gazed out over the water. The setting sun lit the sky on fire with brilliant colors of red and orange. Logan moved to stand next to her and awareness spiked through her. She reminded herself his proximity meant nothing romantic. It was his job to remain close to her.

Her chest suddenly felt hollow. Loneliness as vast as the Pacific Ocean swallowed her until she felt like she couldn't draw in a breath. Emotion pressed against her throat, her eyes stinging with unshed tears. She was so alone. Yes, she had Inez and Jon, and she loved them both, but they weren't her parents. She missed them so much. Missed the love they had for each other and for her. She wanted a marriage like they had had and was grateful Dax had betrayed her before she'd married him.

"I'm ready to go in," she said, her voice cracking with emotion. Although the sunset was picture-worthy, the tears were coming, and she did not want to have a breakdown in front of Logan. Turning away from him, she started back toward the house.

She wasn't fast enough. Logan caught up to her in a few short strides and stepped in front of her, cutting off her path. "Hey," he said. "Are you okay?"

Weslee made the mistake of looking in his eyes. The unexpected tenderness she saw was her undoing, and a sob broke through, unleashing a flood of tears.

CHAPTER 4

*L*ogan had faced danger many times as a Navy SEAL but dealing with a crying woman made confronting an ISIS cell feel like a walk in the park. He wasn't sure what had happened. One minute he and Weslee were staring at the beautiful sunset, and then the next thing he knew she was sobbing.

Not sure if he should say something or give her a hug, he glanced over his shoulder to gauge how far away the house was. They weren't close enough for him to get immediate help from her housekeeper. He was sure Inez would know what to do.

Rubbing a hand across the base of his neck, he turned back toward Weslee. She'd covered her face with her hands, but it didn't hide the torrent of tears streaming down her face. It was up to him to deal with the situation. Man, he sure wished he had some backup. Unfortunately, he didn't have Inez's number. Calling his mother was out of the question. For one, she was on a cruise with some of her quilting ladies. Secondly, she'd be so excited he was calling about a girl that she'd lose focus.

He certainly couldn't call any of his friends. It was bad enough a couple of Sutton's guys were here doing counter surveillance. They were probably watching the whole thing right now.

"Uh...I'm sorry, Weslee," he said, hoping an apology might help.

"You. Didn't. Do. Anything." She sniffed in between each word, making him feel worse. "I'm. Fine."

She was not fine. She was upset and probably could use a hug. He wasn't a hugger, but his mother was. The pretty girl standing in front of him was not his mother. Hugging her would definitely not be the same.

Shifting his stance, he considered his next move. He'd thought that by wearing the Outside Energy shirt the teasing might eliminate his attraction toward her. He realized how wrong he was about that the moment she'd stepped close to him to tug on the hem of his shirt. Her nearness had hit him square in the chest like a heat-seeking missile striking its target.

She made a quiet noise of distress. Shoot, he had to do something. Slowly, Logan loosely put an arm around her shoulders and patted the side of her arm. If he could prod her forward, then he could get back to the house and have Inez take over. Amazingly, the simple contact did the trick. Weslee's tears subsided as she drew in a shuddering breath.

He was about to suggest they go inside when his plan completely backfired. As gracefully as a dancer, she turned into him, circled her arms around his waist, and pressed her cheek against his chest. Then she started crying again. Not as hard as before, but still crying.

Logan didn't know what to do. His one-armed embrace was kind of awkward. He was holding her but not really since his other arm hung limply to his side. He either needed to let go of her or fully embrace her.

An older woman walked by with her dog and glanced their way. The expression on her face was a mixture of concern and censure. It reminded him of a look his mother had given him a few times over the years. Thinking about the scolding his mom would give him if she were to see him right now, he slowly wrapped his other arm around Weslee and tightened his hold.

Dang, she felt small and soft and smelled unbelievably good, like peaches and cream. An explosion of awareness rocketed through him. He swallowed hard as she snuggled in closer, pressing her fingers against his back. Not sure what to say, or if his voice would work properly, he remained silent and just held her.

He hadn't held a woman that wasn't his mother for a long time. So long he'd forgotten how good it could be. The enticing scent of peaches and cream swirled around him, filling his head with all kinds of thoughts. Faint alarms pinged in his head, warning him of impending danger. He needed to let her go and let someone else do the comforting. Heart thudding inside his chest, he loosened his grasp only to have her nestle in closer.

She let out a small sigh of contentment, giving Logan a sense of male satisfaction he hadn't ever felt before. It wouldn't hurt to hold her for a few more minutes, right? He liked helping people, and this was clearly helping her because she'd nearly stopped crying.

On the downside, Logan's awareness for her increased with each beat of his heart. Tendrils of her long hair brushed against his arms, his bare skin flushing as hot as the blood racing through his veins. Without consciously thinking it through, he slid his fingers through the length of her hair. *Shoot.* It was just as soft and silky as he'd imagined, eliciting another forbidden desire. He wanted to kiss her.

As if she'd read his mind, Weslee lifted her tear-stained face to look at him. Most girls didn't cry pretty. Weslee wasn't one of those girls. Framed by dark, spiky lashes, her eyes glistened like the aquamarine stone representing his birth month. Even her flushed face was appealing. And her lips...her cherry-colored lips were slightly swollen and looked so kissable.

Don't do it, Steele. Kissing her is a very bad idea.

He repeated the edict to himself over and over. It took every ounce of self-discipline the Navy had drilled in his head to release his hold and step away from her.

"Feeling better?" he asked, wincing at the tone of his voice. He sounded like he'd just finished a brutal round of PT.

"Yes." She ran a fingertip under her lower lashes. "I...I'm so embarrassed." Her forehead creased as she pointed to the tear-stains darkening the fabric of his shirt. "I'm so sorry. I'll buy you a new shirt."

"That's not necessary." He thought about the Outdoor Energy shirt he'd stuffed into his duffle bag. She'd been upset about the shirt and not just in a healthy-competitive-way. She'd said there was a story behind her reaction. Perhaps the shirt had been the catalyst for her breakdown. "But I wouldn't mind buying a Ground Zero shirt."

A small smile curved her mouth. "I can help you with that."

"I probably need to buy more than one, since I packed two other Outdoor Energy shirts," he said, purposely mentioning the rival company to see if she would talk to him about what had happened.

Her smile dimmed "You don't have to replace your shirts, Logan." Sighing, she looked down at her feet. "I promise I'm not always this emotional. It's just been...a trying day."

It was the opening he needed, but he still hesitated. Delving into her personal life for anything other than the mission was risky. However, in order to fully protect her, he needed more information than the intel he already had. "Want to talk about it?"

Her head snapped up, and she studied him for a long moment. "I suppose I do need to tell you about Dax."

"Dax?" he asked, wondering what kind of parents would saddle their kid with a name like that.

"Dax Hamilton worked for my daddy." She pushed a loose curl behind one ear. "He was also my fiancé."

"Was?" Logan asked, wondering how recent the breakup had been. He already knew she'd been engaged. Her dossier mentioned a brief engagement, but he'd thought nothing about it since the police had cleared the man as her stalker.

"We ended our engagement shortly after my parents died." She rubbed her lips together and looked out over the ocean. "He emailed me a few hours ago asking me to meet him so we could talk. Apparently, he wants me back."

Logan felt like someone had just dumped a bucket of icy water over him. His gut tightened with unreasonable jealousy as he processed Weslee's words. "Are you going to meet with him?" he asked, keeping his tone even and his expression neutral. As her security detail, he needed to vet anyone wanting to meet with her. As a man...that was more complicated, so he compartmentalized his personal feelings and became her bodyguard.

Weslee started walking, and Logan fell in step beside her. His dislike for her former fiancé intensified with every soft-spoken word that fell from her lips. The guy was a snake, deserting her when she'd needed him most. Not only that, he'd betrayed her further by crossing enemy lines to work for Outdoor Energy. Like any traitor, the man had also taken confidential information from Ground Zero and called it his own.

By the time she finished her tale, Logan understood why Inez had wanted him to dispose of his shirt. On top of everything else, the shirt he'd worn had been designed by Dax, although the original concept had been Weslee's.

"Can't you take legal action against him?" Logan asked.

"Jon is working on it, but his contract has a few clauses added in that protect him." She sighed. "Jon believes the contract is fraudulent. He would've never allowed Daddy to hire Dax with the current contract. But so far he hasn't been able to prove anything."

Logan was good at finding hidden documents, but he would need access to the guy's computer to perform an in-depth search. "Any chance Dax's computer is still at Ground Zero?"

"No, he took it with him." She looked at him sidelong. "You think you could find something on it? Even if he permanently deleted it?"

"If it was ever on his computer then I'll find it."

"Really?" She stopped walking, scrutinizing him with a half-smile. "You don't look like a computer nerd."

Logan's gaze narrowed. "I've never been called a nerd in my life."

She laughed, a soft sound that went straight through him. "No, I'm sure you haven't."

A sudden gust of wind sprayed them with a mist of water. Weslee shivered and shoved her hands into the pocket of her sweatshirt. "We better head back," Logan said, noting the last vestiges of daylight were fading fast. No matter how many eyes his buddies had on them or their surroundings, being out after dark was dangerous.

As they walked back to the house, Logan asked her how

she'd gotten into archery and found out her father had introduced her at a young age. Apparently, she'd been a natural. Instead of being in beauty pageants, Weslee had honed her archery skills until she'd become somewhat of a celebrity in the hunting industry and the face for Ground Zero. Logan wished he could see her in action. The competitive side of him would love to challenge her. He was deadly with a gun, skilled with a knife and was an expert in hand-to-hand combat, but he'd never once picked up a bow and arrow.

"You don't actually hunt, do you?" he asked as they ascended the porch steps. He couldn't reconcile this Southern beauty with hunting.

Pausing on one of the stairs, she turned to face him with one eyebrow raised. "Yes, I hunt. And any meat I obtain doesn't go to waste. Once it's processed, I keep some of it, but the majority is donated to local food banks." A trace of sadness flickered across her features. "Daddy and I used to go every season. I couldn't bring myself to go this past season." She looked wistfully beyond his shoulder. "It isn't the same without him."

He wanted to volunteer to go with her, but chasing bad guys was the only hunting Logan had ever done. "I'm sorry," he said, hoping the moisture gathering in her eyes wasn't the start of another crying session. As much as he'd enjoyed holding her, he didn't like her tears. Tears made him feel helpless. It reminded him too much of the times he'd caught his mother crying after his dad was killed in action.

"Goodness," she said, blinking a few times. "I don't know what is wrong with me tonight." She offered him a genuine smile. "I apologize for all this emotional drama. I promise I'll be back to myself tomorrow."

Weslee went straight to her room, claiming a headache.

Inez and Jon also retired shortly after. Although they'd been here for over a week, they were still on the Eastern time zone.

He glanced at his watch and saw it was way too early for him to hit the sack. Besides, Sutton was sending over a tailor to fit him for his tux. His cell buzzed in his pocket with an incoming text from one of the men he'd called to watch over them. He reported that all was clear and asked if they needed to stick around. Logan sent a reply they were good to go, grateful none of the guys from his SEAL team had been available tonight after all. They would've razzed him about getting too friendly with his client.

The tailor arrived a short time later to take his measurements. It didn't last long, so once he was alone, Logan grabbed his laptop and settled onto one of the oversized leather chairs to do some recon on Ground Zero. He clicked on the about-our-company link and saw a picture of the founder, Marcus Wesley Campbell. He read the brief bio on Mr. Campbell that also named his wife, JoAnne, and their daughter, Weslee Anne. Apparently, his client had been named after both of her parents.

His eyes drifted further down the page that had several pictures of Weslee either dressed in curve-hugging athletic clothing or equally curve-hugging camo. She looked amazing in both, but Logan's vote was for the camo. It was pretty hot, especially the pics with her shooting her bow and arrow.

He forced himself to finish reading the rest of the information about how Marcus had taken the small supplemental company and turned it into a huge corporation by marketing the products to outdoor athletes like hunters and fisherman.

Logan was equally impressed by the amount of charitable contributions the company supported. Weslee's insistence about attending the charity ball made more sense. Marcus

Campbell wasn't the kind of rich daddy that spoiled his daughter with expensive cars, yachts and hosted lavish parties. He and his wife spent most of their time giving away their money to help those in need, especially the families right here in the United States.

Logan had traveled the world, witnessing firsthand the abject poverty people lived in, and wished he could do more than just take out bad guys. The statistics of equally destitute women and children without the basics like food, shelter, and clothing surprised him. It also made him want to help.

He clicked on another page that featured the products available and decided to order a few things, especially since all the proceeds during the month of March were donated to help feed hungry children. It was shocking to know so many children in the United States were going without breakfast or lunch and sometimes dinner.

What started out as an intention to order a few things grew into something more. He spent a lot of money on products and merchandise, but he knew it was for a good cause. Plus, his birthday was in a few weeks, so he'd consider it an early gift to himself. Before closing the page out, he noticed a link for the bone marrow match program. He moved the cursor over the link but didn't get a chance to click on it. One of the men from Sutton's was here to take over the night shift for him. Logan didn't think it was necessary, but Jon wasn't taking any chances if the stalker really had followed Weslee to California. He wanted someone keeping watch 24-7.

The next morning, Logan was up before the sun. He never could sleep in, no matter what time he fell asleep. After making his bed, he dressed in a T-shirt and track pants, intent on doing his PT before Jenkins' shift ended.

Although he could hear activity from upstairs, no one was

on the main floor, except Jenkins. "I'll be back at 0530," he said in a quiet voice. "Everything good?"

Acknowledging Logan with a head nod, he yawned and said, "See you in a few."

Logan hated all-nighters, although skipping one night was nothing compared to the brutal five days of no sleep during the infamous hell week of BUD/S. That training had come in handy because most covert ops he and his team had gone on required no sleep or very little sleep. Thankfully, this security detail provided him with a comfortable bed and good food.

He hit the hard sand at a fast pace, the air chilly and thick with moisture. The scent of the salty ocean filled his nostrils as he ran the lonely stretch of the semi-private beach. Listening to the sound of the waves rolling onto the shore, he focused on his breathing and mentally went over the plans for the day.

Weslee had a meeting with the CEO of a spa and gym that had chains along the entire West Coast. Unique to other combination facilities, Total Works Gym and Spa also had an indoor archery range. Ground Zero sponsored archery tournaments all over the US, and Total Works wanted to offer their clients products from Ground Zero. They hoped the cross promotion would boost membership at the gym and increase Ground Zero's presence in California.

Weslee had received a complimentary pass to experience some of the amenities the spa offered, which she planned on using right after the meeting and the photo shoot. Since Sutton employed several female security agents, he'd assigned one to accompany Weslee, sparing Logan from watching over her while she got a facial, manicure and other girly stuff. She also had an appointment with a hair salon to get ready for the charity ball this evening.

Just thinking about dancing with Weslee made Logan sweat more than he already was. Even though a dance required him to hold her close, he'd keep a respectable distance to help him keep his head clear. Civilian life had obviously made him weak. He would've never allowed any personal feelings to get in the way when he was enlisted.

Weslee made him feel things he'd never felt before. While he hadn't dated much since retiring from the SEALs, the girls he'd gone out with were every bit as beautiful as Weslee, yet none of those girls made his heart pound erratically with merely one touch of the hand.

That made her dangerous. Dangerous because loving someone like her meant the loss would be as detrimental as stepping on an IED. It would shred him to pieces, leaving scars that would last a lifetime. His mother was happy, but she'd never allowed herself to fall in love again. There had been nice men interested in her over the years, but she said she couldn't risk loving someone and then losing them again.

Wiping perspiration from his forehead, he pushed those crazy thoughts out of his mind as he turned around and headed back to the house. Focusing back on the mission, he finished his to-do list. He'd take a quick shower and then relieve Jenkins. Once Weslee was in the hands of a female agent, Logan would scout out the Hotel del Coronado. He needed to know exits and identify secure safe spots if he had to get Weslee out of the line of fire quickly.

He also wanted to go over the list of staff and guests Sutton had already screened. The report had come in early this morning. He'd made a cursory glance, and none of the compiled lists contained any red flags.

Slowing his pace the last few yards, Logan scanned the area around the house. The impending sunrise was lighting the sky in small increments like someone was slowly turning up a light switch dimmer.

Before climbing the porch steps, he took a minute to

stretch and steady his breathing. Movement from inside drew his attention as Weslee opened the blinds and slid the glass door open.

"Good morning," she said, stepping onto the porch.

All of Logan's determination to stay immune to her went up in smoke. She was wearing curve-hugging camo yoga pants and a snug black shirt with the Ground Zero logo imprinted on the front.

CHAPTER 5

*W*eslee was certain she heard Logan's teeth grinding together as Trenton Williams, the CEO of Total Works Gym and Spa, made another not-so-subtle innuendo toward her. The female agent assigned to accompany her at the spa had been delayed, leaving Logan to take on the role as her assistant. She wasn't sure if that was a good thing or not. This deal with Total Works was important, and a grumpy bodyguard might alter the outcome of this meeting. At least he was posing as her assistant and not a possessive boyfriend. Trenton was fit and worked out regularly, but she doubted he was much of a match for a former Navy SEAL.

She appreciated Logan's protection, but this wasn't the first time Weslee had experienced one form or another of sexual harassment in her line of work. Men came onto her all the time, making her very selective about where and when she met for private meetings like this one-on-one meeting with Trenton. Still, it was kind of nice having someone watch out for her. Daddy had always protected her. She'd thought Dax would take over that role but instead of protecting her, he'd stabbed her in the back with his betrayal.

"I think we could be really good together." Trenton's eyes made a slow perusal of her, lingering on her chest. "Have dinner with me tonight, and we can explore all the possibilities." He didn't phrase it as a question. He looked at her directly, leaving no doubt in Weslee's mind that the possibilities he wanted to explore had nothing to do with business.

Before she could decline the offer, Logan did it for her. "Miss Campbell isn't available tonight," he said in an even voice.

Trenton flicked Logan a dismissive glance. His attention focused back on Weslee, one corner of his mouth edging up into a crooked smile. "Is that right?" he asked as if Logan wasn't in the room.

"Thank you for the offer, but I do have a previous engagement that I can't miss." Weslee hoped her refusal didn't change Trenton's mind about doing business with Ground Zero. Having their products available in the Total Gym franchise was a big deal and would give them exposure across the West Coast.

"Perhaps another night?" Trenton asked.

"I'm afraid that won't be possible," Weslee said. "Immediately after the charity event ends I'm flying back to North Carolina."

The man sat back, that crooked smile still on his face. He was movie-star handsome and probably at least twice her age. She could tell he wasn't used to women rejecting him, but the gleam in his dark eyes suggested he was amused by her refusal. Like she was a challenge he intended to conquer. "Are you talking about the Children's Charity Ball?"

"Yes," Weslee said, wondering if he planned on attending

tonight's event. She would never peg Trenton as a philanthropist. A philanderer? Yes, but not one to give away money. "My parents were huge supporters, and I wanted to continue the tradition in honor of their memory."

"Then I look forward to seeing you there," Trenton said. "Total Gym is committed to giving back to the community. Perhaps you can save a dance or two for me?"

She heard Logan shift beside her and hoped he wasn't going to speak for her again. She wasn't sure if she liked his interference or not. He was her bodyguard, but that was it. Despite the crazy attraction she felt for him, she knew a relationship with him was a bad idea. Not only did they live on opposite sides of the country, but she also wasn't ready to get involved with another man. She clearly wasn't as mentally healthy as she'd believed. It had only taken one email from her ex-fiancé to set her off.

Thinking of Dax reminded her that she'd felt an instant attraction for him too. Clearly, she needed a relationship that wasn't all fireworks. When the fireworks fizzled out there was nothing left but smoke.

"I'm happy to hear that Total Gym is involved in humanitarian aid," Weslee said as she scooted back from the table. "I look forward to seeing you this evening," she added, hoping the man wasn't going to pin her down to a commitment. "I'm sure my dance card won't be full."

He got to his feet, a gleam of challenge darkening his eyes. "Good to know," he said, coming around the table to shake her hand. However, when she placed her palm against his, he lifted her hand and pressed a lingering kiss on the back. "Like I said before...I think we could be good together." He kept a hold of her hand, giving her fingers a little squeeze. "Outdoor Energy is eager to get their products into Total Works. I only have room for one line of products, and I'd like it to be Ground Zero."

A cold feeling of dread settled like a stone in the bottom of Weslee's stomach. Dax was always one step behind her. She didn't know how he did it. Unless there was a mole inside the company or he'd hired a PI to follow her around. It was tempting to ask Mr. Williams how recently Outdoor Energy had contacted him. Instead, she offered him a bright smile. "I'd like that too." She pulled her hand away. "Thank you for your time. And thank you for the complimentary gift certificate. I'm looking forward to soaking my feet in the mineral footbaths."

"I hope you'll do more than just a pedicure." His eyes traveled the length of her. "We have top masseuses employed here. Ask for the full body massage. I promise you won't regret it."

Weslee kept her smile in place, although she wanted to bolt out of the room. The man had just undressed her with his eyes. She almost wanted to cross her arms over her chest like a shield. "I'll keep that in mind," she said. "Thank you."

She quickly made her way to the exit. Logan held the door open, his face looking fearsome and thunderous. Once she passed through the threshold, he pulled the door closed, placed his hand on her elbow and propelled her forward. "You are not dancing with that slime ball tonight," he said, still seething at the obvious proposition. "And I'm ordering a thorough background on him. He could be your stalker."

"You don't really believe that, do you?" She glanced over her shoulder, grateful that Trenton's door was still closed. "And I don't need you telling me who I can or can't dance with, Mr. Steele."

They rounded a corner, and Logan came to an abrupt stop. "You're wrong about that, Miss Campbell." His eyes flashed with irritation. "It's my job to protect you, so, yes, I will tell you who you can and can't dance with."

For some reason, his declaration made her frustrated. She felt trapped again. "I can fire you, you know," she said with equal irritation.

"Mr. Curtis hired me, not you." Logan's eyes narrowed. "As your boyfriend, I might add."

"Maybe I don't want a boyfriend." *Need.* She had meant to say she didn't need a boyfriend, not want. Before she could launch another argument, the hard lines in his face softened. "Weslee, I'm only trying to protect you. Trenton Williams is a player. The intel I have on him indicates he's had multiple affairs with women of all ages, regardless of their marital status. Aside from his shady morals, my gut instinct says you need to steer clear of him."

Weslee couldn't argue with that. Her instincts were screaming the same thing, but now that Outdoor Energy was vying for the same contract, she couldn't turn her back just because some man had made advances toward her.

"I'm not stupid or naïve," she said, toning down the annoyance in her voice. "Regardless of someone's reputation, I make it a practice to never go to a meeting without bringing Jon or one of my assistants with me."

His blue eyes studied her with an intensity that went straight through her. Finally, he nodded his head. "Good."

Good? That's all he had to say? It was silly to want more from him. Sillier still that she looked forward to him playing the role of her boyfriend.

He's only here to protect you. She needed to remember that this evening. Dancing with him was going to be torture. She already knew how it felt to be in those impressive arms of his.

He pulled his phone from his pocket and stared at the screen. "Your security agent is here." He kept his head bent and typed in a quick reply. "She's meeting us at the front desk." He placed his hand on her elbow again to nudge her forward. His touch sparked a heated awareness as if he had a direct line to every womanly cell in her body. She pulled her arm away just to think straight again.

They reached the front desk, and Weslee was introduced to her new security agent, Kate Bradley. She was far too cute to be a bodyguard. How could someone so petite actually protect her?

"I know what you're thinking," Kate said with a wide smile. "How can she protect me, right?"

"I'm sorry," Weslee said. "I know what it's like to be stereotyped."

"No worries." Kate winked at her. "I'm a black belt in Jiu-Jitsu. Just last night I took down a three-hundred-pound guy." She rubbed the back of her neck. "I'm stoked about this assignment. I could really use a massage."

Weslee laughed, liking her new bodyguard. "Let's go get pampered."

"Have Miss Campbell back at the house by 1730," Logan said. "I have a feeling traffic is going to be backed up."

"Traffic is always backed up," Kate said with an easy smile. "I'll have her back in plenty of time, Steele."

The pampering was exactly what Weslee needed. Kate was a lot more talkative than Logan. It was like having a best friend with her. Something Weslee hadn't had for a while now. In her grief, she'd shut out her friends until they stopped trying to contact her.

Weslee made it home within in minutes of Logan's request. He was on the back deck talking on his phone and didn't appear to be ready for the ball unless he planned on escorting her in track pants and a tight T-shirt, which he looked very good in. Before he turned and caught her eyeing him, she went up to her room to finish getting ready while Kate went outside to talk with Logan.

With her hair fixed in a fancy updo, Weslee felt like a princess when she slipped into the coral colored evening gown. The silky material wrapped around her body with a rounded neckline that showed only a hint of her curves. Sheer material created a cowl-back bodice that flowed into a straight-cut maxi skirt.

"My goodness, you're beautiful," Inez said, indicating for Weslee to turn around so she could make sure the backless bra wasn't visible. "Mr. Logan is going to have a hard time keeping his eyes off you." Inez made a tisking noise. "Maybe he isn't the best choice for a bodyguard tonight."

"I thought you said he was my destiny?" Weslee teased. She turned to look in the full-length mirror and caught her nanny's eye. "Or have you changed your mind?"

"I have not changed my mind, Miss Smarty Pants. I still believe he's meant for you." She fanned herself with her hand. "Trust me, sugar. When you see him in his tux, I think you'll agree with me."

Weslee didn't need to hear about how good Logan looked in a tux. She was already nervous enough. "By the way," she said, opening a silver clutch to put a tube of lip gloss in it as well as her cell phone, "I found out that Kate is also attending the ball tonight so I'll have double the protection."

"Good," Inez said with a grin. "Like I said, Mr. Logan isn't going to take his eyes off you."

"Good thing keeping watch over me is his job then," Weslee said with a light laugh.

"I've known you your entire life, young lady," Inez said, waggling a finger in front of her face. "And you only deflect when you don't want to admit the truth."

Inez did know her all too well so she didn't bother

disputing the claim. Still, regardless of her former nanny's predisposition for romance, Weslee was determined not to let her imagination get caught up in romantic fantasies.

She kissed the older woman's smooth cheek. "Thank you for helping me get ready."

"You're welcome." Smiling affectionately, Inez turned Weslee around and gave her a little push out the door. "Go on now. And please try to have some fun."

Logan waited for her at the bottom of the stairs, looking dangerous and devastatingly handsome in his tux. The cut of the dark suit molded to his body perfectly, enhancing his already impressive physique. His dark hair still looked a little damp from a recent shower, his clean-shaven jaw appealing to her more than it should. It wasn't fair that he looked so good. Even with the serious expression on his face, he was, quite honestly, a beautiful man.

Those cobalt eyes tracked her as she carefully descended the stairs, making Weslee feel cold and hot all at the same time.

"You look very beautiful, Miss Campbell," he said in a low voice.

"Thank you." She smoothed a hand down the front of her skirt. "I haven't dressed up in so long I almost feel like Cinderella going to the ball."

"That would make you her prince charming," Inez said to Logan. "Just don't let her run away at midnight."

A muscle worked in his cheek as he shifted his focus to Inez. "Yes, ma'am. I promise I won't let that happen."

Jon came forward and kissed Weslee on the forehead. "You look just like your mother," he said, his voice cracking with emotion. "She and Marcus would be so proud of you."

"That means a lot to me," Weslee said in a shaky voice. "She was the most beautiful woman in the south so I appreciate the compliment."

Jon turned to Logan. "I hope you're prepared to play the role of her boyfriend and thwart off any unsavory men," he said, sounding very much like a father. "Money doesn't necessarily mean they have manners or morals."

"I'm very aware of that, sir." A hint of amusement touched Logan's mouth as he directed his attention back on her. "Miss Campbell and I have already discussed this. She's promised to only dance with those men that I approve of."

They talked like she was a little girl, not a grown, independent woman. "I didn't exactly promise—" Both men looked at her sharply, cutting her off mid-sentence. She rubbed her lips together. "Of course, I'll take his advice into consideration, but he does not need to act like he's my boyfriend."

The last threads of humor disappeared from Logan's face, making him look downright dangerous. "I'll play whatever role needed to make sure you're safe." He turned and addressed Jon. "If I believe she's in any danger at any time, sir, then we'll leave immediately."

Weslee felt it was wise not to argue any further. Like Cinderella, she didn't want to miss the ball because she was locked in her room. Waving goodbye, she and Logan exited through the front door.

Logan's brooding demeanor reminded Weslee this wasn't a real date as he helped her into his SUV. For safety, he insisted on driving his own car. At least they wouldn't be stuck in the back of a limo, staring at one another in silence.

They drove for a few miles without speaking to one another. It wasn't a comfortable silence like the kind couples experience. Instead, each passing second made the tension grow tighter and tighter until she was sure something would snap.

Once they were on the Coronado Bridge, Logan finally spoke. "You were just messing with me in there, right?"

"I wasn't messing with you," she said, knowing there was a difference between rebellion and independence. "I promise I'll take your advice into consideration, but I don't want to appear anti-social. This event was important to my parents. People knew them well and loved them. I want to carry on their legacy, and refusing to dance with someone could have negative effects on potential donors."

Lips pressed firmly together, Logan focused on the road. Traffic was heavy, and when they were barely crawling along, he glanced her way. "I'll try to keep your feelings in mind, but like I told Mr. Curtis...I'll do whatever it takes to ensure your safety."

"Thank you." She wanted to tell him that she would cooperate with him. Both he and Kate took their job of protecting her seriously. She didn't want anything to happen to them, knowing they would put their lives on the line to keep her safe.

They finally arrived at the Hotel del Coronado. The beautiful wooden structure was like a beacon in the night, glowing with activity. Men and women, dressed like they were on the red carpet for a Hollywood premiere, lined the walkway to the entrance.

A parking attendant waved them over to a waiting valet. Logan left the car idling before he climbed out and accepted the claim ticket. Looking like a movie star, Logan slowly scanned their surroundings before coming around to open the door for her.

"Thank you," she said, placing her hand in his. A zing of heat spiraled from the contact spot and traveled through her body like an electric current. The intensity took her by surprise, making her want to snatch her hand back. Without looking directly at Logan, she climbed out of the car. She didn't need him to see how the simple touch of his hand affected her.

A group of photographers were on one side of the walkway, kept back by a temporary barrier and some fierce looking guards. Logan placed his hand on her lower back and urged her forward, making her feel both flustered and safe.

As they slowly made their way toward the entrance, Weslee regretted her earlier behavior. She'd acted like a spoiled brat when all he was trying to do was keep her out of harm's way. Her mother had raised her to be a lady, and she needed to make an apology.

She tipped her face up to look at him and realized now was not the time to apologize. Focused and stern looking, Logan honed in on the crowd around them. With his attention riveted on their surroundings, it gave her a moment to really study him. His appearance was a little deceiving. The clean-cut look gave him a hot-boy-next-door kind of vibe. Dressed in the expensive tux, he looked more like a sexy British spy than a SEAL. It was his piercing blue eyes that gave him an edge, making him look cool, calm, and dangerous.

As if he knew she was checking him out, his eyes flashed to hers. Glimmering like chips of ice, they held very little warmth and were deadly serious. Still, despite his cool assessment, she felt that magnetic pull toward him. Instead of shrinking away, no doubt what he intended her to do, she held his gaze and gave him a soft smile.

Then she saw it. A fiery attraction flickered behind his eyes just before he shuttered it and looked away. That brief second of intense heat wrapped around her like a warm blanket right out of the dryer. What if Inez was right? What if meeting Logan was her destiny?

CHAPTER 6

*L*ogan should have never looked at Weslee. That dress she had on was driving him crazy, accentuating her soft curves and well-toned muscles. The expanse of smooth, tan skin showing in the back didn't help. She was distracting and not at all intimidated by him like most women were when he leveled them with his practiced look of iron. No, instead of looking away, she'd given him a smile that sent heat all the way to his belly to simmer there. He was growing warmer by the second and wanted to take his jacket off, but that would reveal the gun strapped to his side.

"Good evening folks," the greeter at the door said with a large smile. "Welcome to the Hotel del Coronado."

"Thank you," Logan said, handing over their tickets.

The man found their names on his iPad and tapped on the screen. "Enjoy your evening," he said, handing Logan a map and itinerary of the evening's events.

Logan scanned the paper briefly, making sure nothing had changed since his scouting mission earlier this afternoon.

Weslee leaned in close to him to look at the paper, her scent swirling around him.

"As hungry as I am, I'd like to see the auction items first." She looked at him with a wry expression. "If that's okay with you?"

She wasn't seriously asking for permission. They both knew if he told her no she would do it anyway. "Sounds good."

"Okay then," she said, her full lips lifting into a smile that stole his breath, "lead the way."

Logan held her gaze for a few heartbeats. What was it about this girl that made him feel like this? It knocked him off-balance, and he didn't like it. Heck, this was exactly what had happened to Blaine. The tough as nails SEAL team member had fallen for a girl the instant he'd met her. Logan had vowed that would never happen to him. He wanted to put some distance between the two of them, but staying by her side was part of the job.

"Will the food be any good?" he asked as they navigated their way to the Crown Room. At fifteen thousand dollars per plate it better at least be palatable. Rich people's food tastes were questionable to him. He'd take a juicy hamburger over expensive fish eggs or cooked snails any day.

"I sure hope so because I am hungry."

"You already mentioned that," he said wryly. Most girls he'd dated didn't like to eat in front of him. They nibbled on carrots and lettuce and refused to eat dessert. "Didn't you get something to eat at the gym?"

"I had a Ground Zero protein shake, but that was hours ago."

"Which flavor?" he asked, trying to remember what he'd ordered.

"Birthday Cake." She placed a hand over her stomach. "It's our newest flavor, and it was delicious."

"Hmm, guess I'll have to give it a try. I'm boring and ordered chocolate and vanilla."

She stopped and put her hand on his arm. "You ordered products from Ground Zero?"

He glanced down at his arm where her slender fingers touched the outside of his suit coat. Warmth seeped through the layers of clothing as if she directly touched his skin. Swallowing, he looked at her and nodded. "Yeah, I thought I should try it out."

He'd seen her smile before, but the smile she gave him now lit up her eyes. "Logan, you didn't need to order anything. I could've given you whatever products you wanted to try."

"Thanks, but I thought the proceeds for this month's orders are donated to help feed children?" He shrugged. "I know it isn't much, but hopefully my order will help a little."

"That is so sweet," she said in that soft southern drawl of hers.

Sweet? Had anyone ever referred to him as sweet? He didn't think so. Not even his mother that he could recall. "We better keep moving," he said, not liking all her attention focused on him. It made his tie feel more like a noose around his neck.

The Crown Room, known for its chandelier shaped like a king's crown, wasn't as crowded as Logan thought it would be. That was a good thing. It made his job a lot easier since Weslee drew attention the moment she stepped into the room. Logan learned quickly just how big of a rock he'd been under when he hadn't known who Weslee was. Men, of all ages, knew her and wanted to talk to her. She even had a few female fans.

So far nobody had done or said anything threatening or inappropriate. Even the men who clearly were enamored with her remained respectful. Most of the older generation knew her parents and offered Weslee condolences, happy she was carrying on the legacy of her mother and father.

The only person Logan recognized was his co-worker. He saw Kate across the room, acknowledging her with a slight nod of his chin. The agent looked pretty good dressed in a silver evening gown with a slit up one side that went all the way to her thigh. Knowing Kate, he figured the slit was for practical purposes only. Her Jiu-Jitsu skills were a force to be reckoned with.

A server walked by and handed him a list of the auction items. Ground Zero had several packages up for auction, including one with a trip for two to New Zealand for a national archery championship tournament held annually there. Most of the other packages were valued at a few thousand dollars, which included Ground Zero gear like shirts, hats, and specialty thermoses, along with a variety of products and a top-of-the-line archery combo pack.

As Weslee chatted with other patrons, Logan continued scanning the room, looking for anyone suspicious. Even though the stalker hadn't sent any new messages, and it was doubtful he was the type who could afford attending an event like this, Logan remained vigilant.

At least Trenton Williams wasn't coming. Just before leaving, he'd sent Weslee flowers along with a message that he wouldn't be able to make it to tonight's event. It was a good thing he wasn't coming. Logan didn't like the guy. He didn't trust him either. Just the thought of him slow dancing with Weslee sparked his protectiveness to a new level.

Weslee's laugh drew his attention. Talking with an older couple, she had her back turned to him. Her smooth skin called to him like a siren and sparked a whole new level of possessiveness. He didn't want Trenton Williams or any other man touching her tonight. Logan was feeling more and more like a jealous boyfriend despite her insistence he didn't need to.

Glancing away, he found Kate watching him with an amused expression on her face. The agent lifted an eyebrow like she knew exactly what he was thinking. Before he could cut her a scathing glare, she disappeared into the crowd of people standing near the entrance. He heard a few gasps as the onlookers strained to peer around each other to see who was coming inside the room.

Almost on cue, a hush fell over the gathering as patrons parted as the Red Sea had for Moses. Logan felt a shift in the level of energy from the gathered crowd as if a real king had entered the royal room. He placed a protective hand against Weslee's lower back, his fingertips brushing her bare skin in the process. Having morphed into what he called his SEAL mode, he didn't react to the brief contact. Weslee was once again the mission.

Her body stilled, and she sucked in a quick breath. Logan didn't know if it was due to his touch or if she'd caught sight of the new mystery guest. Right now he didn't care. While he recalled the secure place he'd scouted out today and the quickest route to get her there, he mentally went over the guest list. He didn't remember reading any names he'd consider famous enough for this kind of revered reaction.

It all made sense the moment Logan got a glimpse of the newcomer. Dallin Morrison was nearly as famous in America as Prince William was in Great Britain. The only son to Senator Rand Morrison, one of the longest standing senators in Washington and former vice-presidential candidate during the previous election, Dallin was ready to follow in his father's footsteps. He'd recently announced his intention to replace Senator Morrison when he retired at the end of his term in two years.

The thirty-six-year-old widower was well known for his philanthropy work, patriotism, and his love of the outdoors.

He was personable wherever he went, never coming across as arrogant or entitled due to his family's legacy and wealth. He frequently was the first person to arrive at a disaster, working right alongside the locals to help restore their living conditions.

Everyone loved him, especially the women, each one hoping they'd get to be the lucky lady to mend his broken heart and be a mother to his six-year-old daughter.

Logan could almost guarantee he wasn't Weslee's stalker. So why did he feel this overwhelming sense that he needed to keep her away from the man? The muscles in his shoulders tensed as the future senator drew closer. Logan respected the guy and had always liked him. At least he *had* liked him until Dallin Morrison locked eyes on Weslee and headed straight for her.

CHAPTER 7

*F*rozen in place, Weslee tried to gather her wits as Dallin Morrison approached her. The man was like American royalty and incredibly handsome, looking like a younger version of George Clooney and Ryan Reynolds mixed together. However, the wealthy rancher turned politician wasn't the reason Weslee could barely think straight, let alone breathe.

No, the blame for her temporary bout of senselessness rested solely on her bodyguard and his hand planted on her lower back. His fingers pressed more firmly against her as he stepped closer to her side, thankfully only coming into contact with the fabric of her dress. Her skin still burned where his fingers had briefly touched her.

Dallin was heading straight for her. While she didn't know him personally, she knew he'd recently become a fan of Ground Zero. Over the past six months, he had frequently posted pics to his Instagram account of him fishing, hiking or working out while wearing a Ground Zero shirt and hat.

Blake, one of the marketing guys in charge of handling VIP

customers, had made a connection with Dallin at one of the archery tournaments Weslee had missed during her time off to grieve for her parents. More than once, Blake had told her that Mr. Morrison wanted to meet her in person. Apparently, that meeting was going to take place right now.

Logan dropped his hand and stepped partially in front of her. Dallin didn't seem to notice him, his eyes strictly on Weslee. "Miss Campbell," he said, holding out his hand. "I'm Dallin Morrison and it's a pleasure to finally meet you in person."

"Thank you, Mr. Morrison," she said, placing her hand in his. "It's nice to meet you too." His hand was warm and slightly callused, confirming he knew how to work. His mocha colored eyes regarded her warmly and with open admiration, yet not one single butterfly danced in her stomach.

"Please," he said, giving her hand a little squeeze, "call me Dallin."

"All right, Dallin." She pulled her hand free. "But only if you call me Weslee."

"Weslee." He smiled again, slipping his hands into his pockets. "I understand you were named after your father."

"Yes. It was his middle name." Unwanted emotion blurred her vision at the mention of her daddy. She blinked, clearing away the moisture. A captive audience surrounded them and she didn't want to embarrass herself by crying.

"I'm very sorry for your loss." Compassion sobered his features. This man was no stranger to grief. He'd lost his wife to a fast-growing brain tumor shortly after the birth of their daughter. "I know your parents were both proponents of humanitarian work."

"Thank you," she said, licking her lips. "Helping the less fortunate was their passion."

"I know. It's one of the reasons I was introduced to Ground

Zero." He pulled his hands free and patted his flat stomach. "Your products work too. Helped me lose the few pounds I always manage to put on during the winter."

"He's convinced me," a woman whispered loudly. She nudged her husband in the side. "Bid high on the Ground Zero packages, Albert."

Dallin flashed the couple a white-toothed smile. "You won't be sorry," he said, giving the woman a wink. "Everything tastes amazing too."

The murmuring crowd dispersed, heading toward the auction tables. Weslee shook her head in amazement. "You probably just tripled the amount of money the auctions will go for."

"Good." He considered her for a long moment, his brown eyes thoughtful as if contemplating something serious. "Would you—"

His question was interrupted by a booming voice thanking everyone for coming out to support such an important cause and announcing the auction would begin in a few minutes.

"Before we get started, I'd like to have Mr. Dallin Morrison say a few words."

Surprise flitted across Dallin's face but he quickly hid it behind a smile. Obviously, he hadn't planned on giving a speech, making Weslee wonder why he'd come tonight. Surely he hadn't come just to meet her.

Dallin met Weslee's eyes, giving her a slight nod of his head before he excused himself. While he worked his way up to the podium, the MC talked about Dallin being a last-minute guest and thanked him for his support. He went on to praise Dallin for his humanitarian work, mentioning that he was going to run for the Senate when his father retired.

So his appearance was all for politics. She felt silly for thinking it had anything to do with her. Not that she was interested in dating someone like Dallin Morrison. Although she found him attractive and knew he was a good man, she didn't feel any kind of spark around him, but maybe that was a good thing. No fireworks meant stability. Chemistry didn't necessarily lead to long-lasting relationships.

It's why she kept shooting down Robbie Whitaker, even though at one time she would've jumped at the chance to go out with him. Robbie's parents owned the beach house next to theirs on Emerald Isle. He was their only child and was the quintessential spoiled rich boy, blessed with unbelievably good looks and a charming personality.

Weslee had fallen in love with him the first time she met him. She'd been fifteen and he was twenty-six. Mature for her age and blessed with curves most women never achieved without the help of surgical implants, Robbie noticed her and had flirted with her, even though he had a serious girlfriend. Aside from the vast age difference, Robbie was also a single dad to an eight-year-old son he'd fathered his senior year of high school. It was kind of weird that she was closer in age to his son, Josh, than she was to Robbie. By the time Weslee was old enough to finally date Robbie, the man was married to wife two. She'd also gotten smarter about the kind of man he was.

Although he'd grown even more handsome with each passing year and still charmed her, she was too smart to fall for someone like him. Apparently, he'd just divorced wife number four, and he had decided that it was about time he and Weslee officially went out on a date to explore their mutual attraction. Yes, he'd actually texted her that, along with continually begging her to return to the Emerald Isle house. He and Josh were living with the Mr. and Mrs. Whitaker while their house was under construction. Robbie was building a huge home a few miles down the coastline and couldn't wait to show it to Weslee.

His text messages always made her laugh because his pick-up lines were so cliché. She had to admit that part of her was flattered even though she knew he was a total player. Over the past month, he'd been pretty consistent about wanting to go out with her, telling her he refused to go out with any other women until she at least gave him a chance. Her responses weren't as flirtatious, which made him think she was playing hard to get. She just didn't want to encourage him since her crush had faded over the years.

Logan made her jump when he lightly touched his hand to her elbow. She'd been so lost in thought that she'd missed Dallin's opening statement.

"Sorry," Logan said, having to lean in close to her ear to be heard over the applause for the future senator. His warm breath started a cascade of shivers that awakened the dormant butterflies in her stomach, making them go wild again. "I didn't mean to startle you."

She turned to assure him he hadn't startled her and their mouths nearly collided. "Oh," she said, moving away from him. "You're fine…I mean, I'm fine."

One corner of his mouth edged up. "Good to know," Logan whispered, now that the crowd had quieted in order to hear Dallin speak. "And I think you're fine too."

Weslee narrowed her eyes, wanting to clarify that she'd just been tongue-tied. She hadn't meant to call him fine in a I-think-you're-hot kind of fine. Except…she did think that.

Something dark flickered in Logan's eyes as Dallin said something that made everyone chuckle. "I believe Mr. Morrison thinks you're *exceptionally* fine." His eyes lingered on hers. "I'm not sure I liked the way he looked at you."

"How did he look at me?" she asked. "Surely you don't believe he poses a threat?"

A shadow crossed Logan's face as a muscle in his jaw

ticked. "No, ma'am," he said, edging back ever so slightly. "I don't believe he poses a threat to you."

Weslee got the feeling his answer had a double meaning and wanted to press him further, but he was no longer looking at her. He was all business now, like a Navy SEAL on his watch. She tuned in to Dallin's voice. He encouraged everyone to be generous with their donations, reminding the crowd that children were the future.

The auction began shortly after Dallin ended his impassioned speech. At the auctioneer's request, the future senator remained on the podium. It was a smart move. Dallin motivated people to make substantial bids. Weslee was sure the event would end up bringing in more money than it had in the past.

Throughout the auction, Logan remained aloof and serious, managing to look sexy and brooding while he was at it. He was so focused that he didn't seem to notice all the admiring glances many of the female patrons were giving him. Weslee noticed though...and it bothered her. Bothered her so much that she found herself wanting to inch closer and closer. Maybe she would slip her hand in his to send out the message that he was hers.

Except he wasn't hers. He was her bodyguard.

As the auction came to a close, her stomach was a jumbled mess of angst, envy, and hunger. She placed her hand on Logan's forearm. His muscles were tense and she felt like she'd latched onto a slab of marble. "Are you as hungry as I am?" she asked when he looked down at her.

A slow smile curved his lips. "I guess you could say that."

Weslee tried not reading anything into his sexy smile or the possible innuendo, but she liked the way he was looking at her and hoped the other women eyeing him got the message they were together. She wished she hadn't made such a big fuss about him not being her boyfriend. It was too late to tell him she'd changed her mind.

"Okay." She tightened her hold on his arm. "We should get something to eat before the dance starts."

"Sounds good to me."

They made their way to the buffet tables, Weslee clutching the fabric of his sleeve in an effort to remain close to him. She was fully aware of the two women trailing behind them. They had openly admired Logan and didn't have any qualms about following him.

The buffet held a variety of delicious food. Logan handed her a plate, forcing her to let go of him. "This actually looks edible," he said, choosing a variety of gourmet appetizers.

Weslee added a few things, but her appetite wasn't nearly as healthy as his. The two women who had followed them to the buffet table had their eyes trained on Logan as if he was on the menu and they wanted a large helping. Again she questioned why she had made such a fuss about him posing as her boyfriend. Now, if she danced with anyone else, Logan would be free to dance too. She didn't like thinking about him dancing with anyone else but her.

Dallin Morrison single-handedly ensured the auction items sold at a premium price, so there wasn't really a need to stay for the dance. Except for the opportunity to dance with Logan. She may never get the chance again.

She glanced at the two women who had moved to the end of the table near the desserts. They had no intention of indulging in the delicious sweets. Both of them looked like scarecrows with big boobs. Anyone that emaciated would not be so well-endowed without the help from a plastic surgeon. No, the women were here for one thing. Her bodyguard.

A knot of possessiveness twisted inside her stomach. On impulse, she edged around Logan, purposely brushing her arm against his as she did so. It was shameful, really, to use physical contact like a weapon. Especially for a southern girl who had been reared to be a lady from the time she'd learned to walk. Hopefully she emitted the same magnitude of electricity with her touch as he did with his, otherwise, he'd think she just wanted to get to the desserts before he did.

"My goodness, I don't think you have any room for dessert," she said with a light laugh. "We better find a table to eat at and then come back if you still have room."

An amused expression crossed his face. "Thanks, but there's always room for dessert." He looked over her head to where the two women waited. A crooked smile appeared on his handsome face as he looked back at Weslee. "I might even get two."

A pit formed in her stomach. He was referring to the dessert, right? "I hope you don't make yourself sick," she said, not sure where all this craziness was coming from. "Too much sugar is bad for you."

His grin widened. "I'll keep that in mind."

They moved in tandem, Weslee determined to stay in front of him. Logan made a move similar to hers as he went around her except he didn't touch her in the process. "Hello, ladies," he said to his admirers. "Any recommendations for dessert?"

Hearing him flirt made the pit in her stomach open up as wide as the Grand Canyon. Jealousy was a horrible feeling. She had never experienced it quite at this level. What did that mean? She'd known Logan Steele for only a few days. Not even long enough to develop a healthy crush, yet she was ready to get into a fight with two women just for looking at him.

One of the girls laughed a deep, throaty laugh like she was a smoker. "I have a few ideas you might like," she said in a husky voice. "Depends on how big of an appetite you have."

The suggestive tone made Weslee sick to her stomach with

jealousy. Too afraid Logan might actually flirt back, she couldn't look at him and needed to leave. Abandoning her plate, she lifted her skirt up and turned to walk away.

Logan's hand circled her wrist like a manacle. How dare he make her stay and listen to the women openly proposition him. "Oh, it's not for me," he said, gently tightening his hold when she tried to free herself. "It's for my girlfriend."

CHAPTER 8

Fighting back a smile, Logan gripped onto Weslee's wrist and felt her go perfectly still. Jealousy radiated off of her like the fallout from a nuclear bomb. It settled a bit as she drew in a sharp breath. When he was sure she wasn't going to bolt on him, he slid his palm down, threaded their fingers together and pulled her next to him. "What sounds good to you, babe?" he asked, giving her fingers a little squeeze.

Weslee remained stiff. She needed to loosen up and play the part of his girlfriend or the two women standing in front of him weren't going to buy it. He rubbed his thumb across her skin. "Want me to pick something for you?" he asked, giving her a wink.

That did the trick. As if a director had just called out *action*, amusement sparkled in her eyes and a tiny smile emerged. "Would you, sweetheart?" she said, playing up her southern accent. "I swear I can never make up my mind."

She was playing the part a little too well. The pout on her lips tempted Logan to lean down and kiss her. He forced his eyes away from her mouth and turned to look over the dessert choices. He caught the dark-haired woman who had come onto him eyeing Weslee viciously as if she were her competition. Weslee was so far out of this chick's league it wasn't even a close race. The woman's redheaded companion still watched Logan like a vulture ready to swoop in to devour her prey. She didn't care if he had a girlfriend or not. Heck, more than likely she'd invite Weslee to come along.

Women like these two had never appealed to him. Sex was like a form of entertainment to them. No commitment. No tender feelings of love. Just an activity meant to satisfy their desires. Logan's mother had raised him to respect girls. He didn't mess around and he hated guys who used women and then tossed them aside like an empty beer can.

Wanting to get away from the duo, he chose a decadent chocolate cheesecake garnished with fresh raspberries. Reluctantly, he let go of Weslee's hand to pick it up. "Ladies," he said, holding up the plate, "I think I've made my choice."

The brunette lasered him with a disdainful expression while the redhead smiled and lifted one shoulder up in a shrug. "I hope you enjoy it."

"We will," Weslee said, wrapping her hand around his arm. "Y'all have a good night." Then she picked up her abandoned plate with her free hand and the two of them walked away.

A few tables were scattered near the windows. Logan led them to a table closest to an exit. He nodded his head at Kate, who breezed by them on her way to the buffet table. Seeing the fellow security agent reminded him he still had a job to do.

"You did good back there, Campbell," he said, trying to get his mind back into the op.

"Campbell?" she asked, nudging his arm. "What happened to babe?"

Her comment made him laugh. "So, babe isn't a term of

endearment I can use?" he asked, unloading the two plates onto the table.

"I didn't say that. I think you used it very appropriately." She set her plate down and narrowed her gaze. "I had a few names I wanted to call those women, but my mama taught me it's not ladylike to speak like that, especially in polite company."

He laughed again. "Weslee, I've been in the military for the past ten years. Pretty sure whatever you have to say isn't going to offend me." He pulled out a chair for her. "Even my mother would approve in this case."

"I suppose so." She smiled and slid onto the chair. "Thank you."

Logan's hands rested on the back of the chair, ready to help her slide closer to the table. But his view from behind her was so incredible that he couldn't move. With her hair piled on top of her head, it left her slender neck bare, exposing soft skin he'd like to brush his lips across.

"Everything okay?" she asked, angling her face to look at him.

"Yes, ma'am," he said, careful not to touch her as he slid the chair closer. He knew being so acutely aware of her, one touch of her skin would be like touching a tripwire, setting off a massive explosion.

He took the seat opposite of her, positioning his chair to give him a view of the room and the people milling around. So far the only one stalking Weslee was Logan.

He picked up the white cloth napkin that held the utensils and unrolled it. A curse word nearly slipped out when he spied Dallin Morrison coming across the floor toward them.

"Pardon me for interrupting," Dallin said as he approached their table. "I wanted to apologize for ending our conversation so abruptly. I didn't know they were going to call on me to speak."

"No need to apologize, Mr. Morrison," Weslee said, smoothing the cloth napkin with her fingers. "You were wonderful. I'm certain they raised more money because of you."

"It's Dallin." He gazed longingly at Weslee, making Logan want to sweep his foot out to knock the man on his backside. "And thank you for the kind words."

Color infused Weslee's cheeks as her eyes cut to Logan for a brief heartbeat. Dallin followed her line of sight and the two men locked eyes. He wasn't exactly challenging Logan, but he was definitely putting feelers out to see where Logan stood. How had he ever liked this guy? Right now he wanted to put the drop on him.

"I don't believe we've met," Dallin said, holding out his hand. "I'm Dallin Morrison."

Scooting his chair back, Logan got to his feet. He maybe had an inch on Dallin and a few pounds he hoped were solid muscle. "Logan Steele," he said, gripping the man's hand just hard enough to let him know he was present.

"It's a pleasure to meet you, Logan." Dallin withdrew his hand, flexing his fingers as he dropped it to his side.

Maybe Logan had gripped a little too hard. "Likewise." Logan sat back down, hoping Weslee didn't ask the guy to join them. Logan stared him down until the guy finally looked away.

"Well, I'll let you eat your meal," he said to Weslee, pausing for a moment as if giving her a chance to ask him to stay. "I hope you'll save a dance for me?"

"Of course," Weslee said, now mutilating her napkin rather than smoothing it out. "You should get a plate. The food is delicious...I mean, I haven't tried anything yet, but it smells very good."

"Thank you. I believe I will." Dallin stepped back and gave her a slight nod of his head. He didn't spare Logan another glance as he headed for the buffet table.

Envy, frustration and white-hot anger tangled inside Logan's chest. He wasn't used to having these kinds of emotions. He'd always thought men who got so twisted up over a woman were weak and they just needed to man-up. He didn't feel weak. It was more primal like he wanted to shout out that Weslee was his woman and to back off.

With all the crazy thoughts racing through his mind, he decided it was better to keep his mouth shut. He wished he could turn his brain off because ideas like putting a ring on Weslee's finger to stake his claim seemed like a perfectly rational thought to him. Logan wasn't the marrying kind of guy. So why was the memory of Blaine's wedding to Elena forcing its way into his mind? Except instead of Blaine as the groom it was Logan standing next to Cannon while he watched his bride glide down the aisle toward him.

The guys, especially Hammerton, would never let him live this down. Logan was the guy who wasn't going to ever fall for a girl. Love was too risky, and he never wanted to put a woman through what his mother had experienced when his dad had passed away. Logan had felt so helpless as a little boy, unable to console his mother.

A voice inside his head reminded him he wasn't in the Navy anymore. Another voice argued that he still liked doing dangerous things like jumping out of airplanes, scaling the side of a mountain and flying helicopters.

Then there was that deep inner voice he tried to ignore. The one reminding him of the dark things he'd seen and done as a SEAL. The shrinks he'd talked with over the years, especially after escaping from the Syrian prison, had helped quiet those voices. Logan was fortunate that he didn't have any signs of PTSD, but he'd experienced bouts of depression. Exercise and staying away from alcohol and drugs had gotten him through those times. Talking with his SEAL team also helped. They got where he was coming from.

But if he ever did get married, his wife would want to know about his time as a SEAL. Sure, most of the ops he'd been on were confidential, but what if she asked him if he'd ever killed someone? That had happened to him a few times by girls he'd gone out with. Logan had always answered that question with the standard *it's classified*, which was true, but they weren't asking him *who* he had killed...just *if* he had killed.

He cracked the end of the lobster tail and dug the meat out, trying not to think about anything that had to do with getting married, but images of Weslee wearing a lacy white wedding dress kept sneaking past his defenses. Curse words his mother would never approve of, no matter what the situation was, flitted through his mind as he called himself stupid for even entertaining the idea of marriage.

He cracked another part of the lobster tail with so much force he crushed the shell into the tender meat.

"What did the lobster ever do to you?" Weslee asked. She was teasing him. Logan liked it when she teased him.

"Not a thing." He looked at her for the first time since Dallin had come in and ruined their date. Okay, so it wasn't exactly a date. Still, he'd messed up their meal.

"Hmm," she said, biting her bottom lip as if trying to suppress a giggle. "Are you by chance projecting?"

"Are you some psychology major or something?" He dropped the ruined lobster tail on his plate and picked up a stuffed mushroom and popped it in his mouth.

"Nope, I majored in business with an emphasis on

marketing." She waited until he looked back up at her. "Now you're deflecting, Lieutenant Steele. Is there something you'd like to talk about?"

His lips twitched. If she knew all the crazy thoughts he had going on in his head that involved her she'd run straight into Dallin Morrison's waiting arms. Logan wasn't husband material. Dallin was every girl's dream come true.

"Nope, I'm good."

"It might help," she said, taking a sip of water. Then she smiled at him, and he knew she liked having the upper hand. Liked keeping him off-balance.

Two could play this game.

"I'm not much of a talker." A wicked grin stole over his face as he purposely looked at her pretty mouth. "I'm more of an action kind of guy."

"Oh." She rubbed her lips together and looked down at her pathetic plate of food. For a girl who claimed to be starving she wasn't eating very much.

"Something wrong with your food?" Logan asked.

"No, I'm saving room for dessert."

Logan's mouth went dry when he met her simmering gaze. *Whoa.* Did she want dessert as in the chocolate cheesecake or was she talking about a metaphorical dessert?

If it was the latter, he knew she wasn't offering what the other women had implied. But Logan was a strong proponent of kissing. He was sure there were a ton of health benefits that came from kissing. Just thinking about pressing his mouth to hers was making him feel pretty good.

Another blush blossomed on her face. "I'm not talking about the same kind of dessert Scarecrow Girls were talking about." She picked up her fork and stabbed a tiny red tomato.

He quirked an amused brow. "Scarecrow Girls?"

"You know what I'm talking about." She continued to stab

the bite-sized tomato with her fork. "And I doubted they believed I was your girlfriend."

"What makes you think that?"

"Because they're watching us." She stared at something over his shoulder. "And we're not exactly acting like we're a couple."

Logan studied her closely. Why did she care about two women flirting with him so much? Was it the same reason he'd wanted to knock America's most eligible bachelor flat on his back a few moments earlier? Things could get so complicated if the two of them acted on their mutual attraction. She met his eyes again, giving him a look that made every one of his senses buzz to life.

Since when did Logan ever do the uncomplicated?

"Will it help if I hold your hand?" he asked, reaching across the table to place his hand over hers that held the fork. "I think you've tortured that tomato enough, anyway."

"Probably," she said, letting the fork go.

Although she agreed with him on the tortured tomato, her one-word reply also answered his first question. The table was small, making it easy to lift her hand to his mouth. "How about this?" he asked, marveling that kissing the back of a woman's hand could feel so sensual.

"That works too," she said in a breathless tone.

He circled his thumb in the center of her palm as he lowered their joined hands back to the table. His eyes drifted down to her mouth. Oh man, he wanted to kiss her. Did rich people kiss each other in public or did they adhere to the no PDA rule?

As he glanced around to see if any other couples were engaged in more than handholding, one of the hosts for the charitable event announced the ballroom was now open for dancing. It was the perfect setup to prove to the Scarecrow

Girls that he and Weslee were a couple. He hoped Dallin Morrison got the message too.

"I'll bet if they saw us dancing they would believe it," he said, suddenly feeling as nervous as he'd been when he'd asked a girl he liked to prom. While the girl in high school had said yes, Weslee might shoot him down.

"I think so too," she said, her voice sounding more breathy than before. "Do you want to go now or wait until after you're done eating?"

His appetite for the delicious food covering his plate had suddenly switched to something else entirely. On the drive to the hotel, she'd put on some kind of tropical-fruit scented lip gloss. Tropical fruit was exactly what Logan was craving right now.

"I'm not that hungry anymore," he said in a rough voice. "What about you?"

Her eyes darted to the chocolate confectionary, lingering for a long moment. Looks like she was going to shoot him down for dessert. The real dessert, not the metaphorical kind.

"Actually," she said almost shyly. "I'm not really a fan of chocolate cheesecake."

A slow smile spread across his face. "Good to know." Keeping a hold of her hand, he stood up and gently tugged her to her feet. "I think I'll let you pick out the next dessert."

Their eyes connected, both of them smiling at each other as if they were the only two people in the room.

"Excuse me," a timid voice said from beside them. Both he and Weslee turned to see a young girl dressed in a typical catering uniform. "I'm really sorry to bother you, Miss Campbell, but I just wanted to say thank you for helping save my little brother's life." The girl gave her a watery smile. "He received a bone marrow transplant that put his leukemia into remission. The donor signed up because of you and your company."

"That's wonderful," Weslee said. "Thank you for telling me."

"Would it be okay if I took a picture with you?" She bit her lip and looked over her shoulder. "I know we aren't supposed to bother the guests, but it would really mean a lot to Jack. That's my little brother's name."

"Of course," Weslee said. "And it's no bother at all."

Before Logan could move out of the way, the girl moved next to Weslee and held up her phone to take a few selfies with him included. "Thank you so much," she said, stepping away and slipping her phone back into her pocket. "Jack is going to be so happy."

"You're welcome." Weslee watched the girl walk away with a smile that lit up her face, making her even more beautiful. "Thanks for being a good sport," she said, giving Logan's hand a squeeze.

"Sure, it wasn't a big deal." The big deal was how kind Weslee was. Logan couldn't help thinking how much his mother would love it if he brought a girl like Weslee home. He also made a mental note to look further into the bone marrow match program to see what he needed to do to sign up.

Leading Weslee across the floor, he purposefully walked past the Scarecrow Girls. He made sure to gaze down at Weslee like he was totally in love with her. It was a little frightening how easily that could be true. If he wasn't careful he could fall in love with Weslee.

They arrived in the ballroom just as a song ended. Some of the couples moved off of the dance floor while others waited for the next song to start. Wanting to be near an exit in case something happened, Logan skirted around the edge of the ballroom until he came to the exit closest to the beach. It was an emergency exit only, which meant there wouldn't be a lot of activity around the door if they needed to make a quick escape.

The next song started as Logan drew Weslee into his arms. Placing one hand at her lower back while holding her right hand in the traditional dance hold, it occurred to him that unless Dallin or the two women had followed them into the ballroom then acting like a couple wasn't really necessary.

He should keep her at a proper distance, but having her in his arms dulled his ability to think clearly. Or it could also be the voltage of electricity zipping between them that had short-circuited his brain. Whatever it was, he didn't care. Weslee's body melted against him as she placed her left hand on his shoulder and nestled her face near the crook of his neck.

A vocalist crooned an Ed Sheeran melody he'd heard before that talked about dancing and falling in love. Logan had always scoffed at such sappy words and usually skipped songs like this, but as he listened to each word he totally got where the songwriter was coming from. The next part of the lyrics made Logan's heart jump to a rate he usually only achieved after sprinting.

But darling, just kiss me slow, your heart is all I own...

The words, though sang softly, seemed to be like a loudspeaker in his ear. He wanted to kiss Weslee long and slow and wished they were dancing in the dark instead of a ballroom with bright chandeliers hanging over them.

Each word penetrated him to his core, and the air in his lungs felt trapped, like if he didn't make a move then his chest would explode under the pressure. When he couldn't stand it anymore, he made a slight adjustment with the angle of his head, bringing the side of his face close enough he could feel her warm breath against his jawline.

Better...but not exactly what he wanted. Blood pounded through his veins, his pulse loud in his ears, making it almost impossible to hear the lyrics. He strained against the throbbing sound, trying to catch the words. He wanted this beautiful girl to be his, and he wanted to be her man.

Swallowing hard, he ached to turn his head and press his lips to hers. Was Weslee feeling any of this or was he the only one losing his mind?

As if she heard his thoughts, she shifted her face until her cheek touched his. Her skin was soft against his jaw as her scent swirled around him in an intoxicating cloud of feelings he'd never experienced before.

Somehow he still managed to keep swaying to the music. Managed to keep breathing as the song continued. Weslee was the first to make the next move, turning her face a little more toward him until their mouths nearly touched.

The next move was all his. A move that felt as dangerous as working the flight deck of an aircraft carrier. Kissing her crossed a line and there would be no going back. While he could pass it off as role-playing, he knew he'd want more than just this kiss. He knew all of this...and yet he wasn't going to let it stop him.

It hadn't been that long since he'd kissed a woman. Jace had set him up with some girl a couple of months ago, and Logan had kissed her goodnight. He'd thought about calling the girl again but never had because there just wasn't any real spark.

The moment his lips touched Weslee's mouth there was more than fireworks. It was like a stick of dynamite exploded inside him, cracking him open and unleashing a starving man. Her lips melded with his in equal passion as he practically devoured her.

A loud popping sound made Logan rip his mouth from hers as he whirled around to move in front of Weslee. While searching for the shooter, he shoved his hand inside his jacket and wrapped his fingers around the handle of his gun.

"Logan," Weslee said, touching his shoulder. "It's just a champagne bottle."

He blinked, zeroed in on a couple standing next to a minibar. A man held up a bottle, laughing as he poured the bubbly liquid into two glasses.

"She said yes!" the man shouted out as he handed his new fiancée a glass of champagne.

As the room erupted in loud applause, Logan drew in a shaky breath and loosened his hold on the gun. Nobody had taken a shot at Weslee. She was safe. And he was an idiot. How could he have allowed himself to get that distracted?

"Sorry about that." He rubbed a hand across the back of his neck and evened out his breathing. "I thought that was a gun." He should apologize for kissing her too.

"Do you really think my stalker would try shooting at me in a public place?"

"Probably not." He scowled. In his line of work, one should never make assumptions. "But that doesn't mean I should have let my guard down." His mood darkened. He should've never kissed her either.

"Logan, you did nothing wrong. The second you heard the noise you were in front of me." Her lower lip trembled, and she looked down at her hands. "I think that scared me more than anything."

"What scared you?" he asked in a low voice.

"You stepped in front of me even though you assumed someone was shooting at me." She lifted her face and looked directly into his eyes. "I don't understand why you'd risk your life for me?"

"That's my job," he said without thinking it through. While that was true...he also cared about her. Really cared about her. And that *scared* him. "I protect people, Weslee. It's what I'm good at." He wanted to add that he was lousy at relationships because he never allowed himself to get close to a woman. His SEAL brothers and his mom were the only people he'd ever let in.

The hurt look in her eyes told him she didn't need him to say it out loud. "I see," she said. "Well, thank you, Lieutenant Steele. If you get yourself killed because of me then I'll feel so much better about it."

She was mad at him again. Good. He needed her mad at him. Wished she would try to fire him again. This time he wouldn't argue with her but call Sutton to get a replacement.

Another song started, this one a little more upbeat. Logan wasn't in the mood to dance again. He couldn't trust himself to keep her at an appropriate distance, and he couldn't properly guard his client. *Client.* He had to think of her as his client otherwise he might drag her off to a dark corner and finish kissing her.

Since they were near the outer edge of the dance floor, he took Weslee by the hand and pulled her along with him until they were no longer where all the dancers were. He wanted to demand they go home right now, but she'd had her heart set on the ball. They could stay longer as long as he watched from the sidelines. At least with her dancing with someone else he was free to keep a vigilant watch on the rest of the patrons.

An image of Dallin Morrison holding Weslee in his arms started a tidal wave of those tangled emotions he couldn't shake. He tamped down the surge of possessiveness as he envisioned Weslee and Morrison dancing close together and kissing.

"I think I'm ready to go home," Weslee said without looking directly at him. "The auction was successful, and that's all I really care about."

Guilt pressed heavy on Logan's shoulders at how relieved he felt. He knew his relief had very little to do with her security detail. He needed to get her home and put some distance between them. Inez had told him not to let Weslee run away, but Logan was the one running.

"Are you sure?" he asked more out of obligation.

"I'm positive." She pulled her phone from her little silver purse and tapped in a message. "I'll tell Jon to notify the pilot that we'll be leaving earlier so he can file a new flight plan."

"Okay," he said, pulling out his phone. "Let me text Agent Bradley to come stay with you while I get the car."

Weslee nodded her head, keeping her gaze averted. He'd hurt her, but it was better now rather than sometime down the road.

Kate arrived almost immediately. "Thank you for calling it an early night," she said to Weslee. "I never wear heels and my feet are killing me."

"Mine too," Weslee said with a sad smile.

Her dejected voice created so much conflict inside Logan that he felt like he couldn't breathe. He wanted to run away while at the same time hold her in his arms. He hadn't lied when he said he was good at protecting people. He'd taken over the role of protecting his mother at a very young age after his dad had been killed. Seeing Weslee distressed upset him, but he couldn't comfort her. Not when he knew what would happen if he did.

"It shouldn't take long to get the car," he said to Kate. "I'll shoot you a text once I have it."

She waved him off, so Logan worked his way through the crowd as quickly as possible. Weslee was in good hands with Kate. Probably safer than with him, since Agent Bradley wasn't distracted by their client the same way he was.

Logan knew what he had to do. While he waited for the valet to bring him his SUV, he typed in a message to Sutton Smith. Before sending the finished text, he read over it again and grimaced. He wasn't a quitter. He'd been known to go rogue if a mission went sideways, improvising and doing whatever it took to complete the op, but he'd never quit.

Decision made, he pushed send. Logan's gut instincts were rarely wrong, and his gut told him that if he got on that private plane with Weslee Campbell, his life would change forever.

CHAPTER 9

*W*eslee settled back into the leather recliner on her father's jet and closed her eyes. Her headache had eased quite a bit, but she longed for the medication to fully take effect so she could put Logan and that unbelievable kiss out of her mind. His kiss had ruined her and her future relationships. No one had ever kissed her like that. Not even her fiancé.

The fiery passion Logan had unleashed inside her in that brief moment had stunned her. She firmly believed that intimacy should be reserved for marriage. She still believed that, but she'd never been so tempted to throw all of that away as she was in that moment of insanity brought on with his kiss. If he'd carried her off to a room, she wasn't sure she had it in her to resist. It scared her to death, and yet she still wanted him.

She heard a noise and thought maybe Logan was here, but it was only the flight attendant fiddling with something in the galley. Her bodyguard hadn't arrived at the airport yet. Honestly, she doubted he would show up at all. Kate had escorted them to the airport after Logan left to take care of some urgent business. Agent Bradley didn't know anything about his emergency. She looked as in the dark as Weslee felt.

Inez settled into the chair beside her. "Honey, there's no reason to fret. Logan will be here. I know he will."

"I'm not fretting." Weslee kept her eyes closed. "I'm tired and still have a headache."

Inez thought the whole reason she had come home early was due to a headache. Heartache was more like it. Logan had kissed her and then passed her off to another agent.

Why had she flirted with him in the first place? She cringed inwardly at how eagerly she'd jumped into the role as his girlfriend. That had been her first mistake. Okay, maybe her first mistake had been how jealous she'd acted when the two floozies had propositioned Logan under the guise of dessert. Then she'd gone and done the same thing. On a much more innocent level, of course. Kissing had been on her mind...until he'd actually kissed her. She was ashamed to admit how easily she could've been swayed for something more.

Nope, she should've never openly flirted with a man like Logan. But after Dallin had stopped by their table and asked her to save a dance for him, Logan had acted like the possessive boyfriend he said he didn't need to portray unless there was a threat. Dallin wasn't a threat to her safety.

Secretly, she'd loved how jealous Logan had been. It had lowered her inhibition, and she'd instigated the flirty banter and then challenged him to show the two women she was really his girlfriend. He'd taken the challenge. Boy, had he taken the challenge. He held and kissed her hand and then asked her to dance.

That dance. A sigh nearly escaped through her lips as she remembered every tiny detail of the dance. The feel of his hand on her lower back, his masculine scent that made her want to bury her face against his neck and breathe him in. His heart had pounded just as furiously as hers as they'd inched their faces closer and closer until their mouths connected in a kiss to transcend all kisses in the history of the world.

Then the pop of a champagne bottle brought them back to reality. Instantaneously, Logan had morphed from the hot-boy-next-door, past the sexy spy, and directly to a fearless SEAL. She still couldn't believe he hadn't even hesitated for a second to protect her. It made him that much harder not to want.

"Is he here yet?" Jon asked, coming out of the restroom. He glanced at his watch. "I'm going to put a call into Sutton if Mr. Steele doesn't arrive in the next five minutes. We're wasting time and resources waiting for him."

"Hush," Inez said. "Our girl still has a headache."

"It's getting a little better," Weslee said, opening her eyes to look at the two people who had never failed her. "I think you should go ahead and call Mr. Smith. Perhaps Agent Bradley can come with us."

Jon settled onto the recliner across the aisle from Inez. "That's not a bad idea," he said, tapping on the screen of his phone to scroll through his contacts.

"Of course it is," Inez said. "I think Miss Kate is a lovely person. She's capable and all, but Mr. Logan, well…I just have a feeling about him."

"Stop playing matchmaker," Jon said. "Mr. Steele's job is to protect Weslee, not woo her."

Since they were talking like she wasn't here, she closed her eyes again and tried thinking about anything but her bodyguard. Why couldn't her fascination be with Dallin Morrison? The man was obviously interested in her, which was absolutely amazing. What woman in the world wouldn't be excited about the billionaire-soon-to-be-a-senator pursuing her? There were even rumors that Dallin would make a bid for the presidency someday. He was the perfect catch. He even came from a big family, something she'd always wanted. Certainly, a man like him could kiss a girl senseless, right?

Then there was Robbie Whitaker, although he wasn't in the running for husband. She didn't want to become another notch on his bedpost or ex-wife number five, but he could be a nice distraction and could probably deliver a good kiss.

Still, no matter how many times she tried to think about someone else, Logan would intrude until he was the only one occupying her mind. She had to stop this madness. No more thinking about Logan or kissing him again. Definitely no more flirting if he happened to show up. Ignoring him was her only option.

"Sutton, Jon Curtis here," Jon said in a loud voice. "Yes, sir, that's exactly why I'm calling."

Weslee couldn't help opening one eye to peek at Jon. She wished he was on speaker phone so she could hear what Mr. Smith was saying. Inez had her head turned as well, so Weslee opened both eyes.

"I see," Jon said, glancing at his watch again. "No, of course not." He listened, his brows furrowed. "Sounds good. Thank you." He ended the call and slipped the phone into the pocket of his dress shirt.

"Well?" Inez asked. "What did you learn?"

"Everything is fine." John slipped on his reading glasses and opened his laptop. "Mr. Steele—"

"Is here," a deep voice said. "I apologize for the delay."

Weslee's stomach dropped to the floor at the sound of Logan's voice. Her entire body felt alive, which irritated her more than when she'd thought he wasn't coming. For the first time since their kiss, she met Logan's eyes. Even at this distance a current of awareness arced between them as if they were connected by a single wire.

Act normal Weslee Campbell, not like some immature debutante.

"You're welcome to choose any seat," Weslee said, hoping her voice wasn't as shaky as her body felt.

"Thank you." He jerked a thumb over his shoulder. "If it's okay, I think I'll join the pilot in the cockpit."

Seriously? She'd hoped he would choose the seat across from her so she could practice ignoring him. Now she was going to think about him for the entire flight home! "I hope you're not going to sweet-talk your way into flying the plane, Mr. Steele. You may have flown a helicopter once before, but they are not the same thing." The second she spoke she wanted to reach out and snatch the words back. She sounded bitter and exactly like a spoiled debutante.

He lifted a questioning brow. "Ma'am, being a sweet talker isn't something I've ever been accused of."

Ha! She'd witnessed firsthand how well he could sweet-talk. She kept her mouth shut as he grinned wider.

"But I can fly more than helicopters."

"Are you a pilot, Mr. Logan?" Inez asked, sounding like he was the world's most gifted man alive.

"Yes, ma'am." His lips twisted into a wry grin. "I even have previous experience on this aircraft. I'm one of Sutton's backup pilots."

"How wonderful," Inez said, turning to look at Weslee. "Isn't that wonderful, Weslee?"

"Mm-hmm," she said, gazing out the window into the dark. "Wonderful."

"Now that we've agreed how wonderful Mr. Steele is, maybe we can take off?" Jon asked. He got cranky when it was past his bedtime, so Weslee didn't point out that she hadn't actually agreed on how wonderful Logan was in general, just that it was wonderful he was a pilot.

She grudgingly admitted to herself it was comforting to know that if anything happened to their pilot they wouldn't die because they had a backup pilot onboard. Although she didn't let it stop her from getting on a plane, she had a fear of flying that stemmed from an incident when she was a child. The plane she and her parents had been on hit severe turbulence not long after taking off, causing the overhead bins to open and dump some of the luggage. She remembered being so terrified, especially from all the screams from the other passengers. The motion sickness medication she always took made her sleepy, which helped curb her anxiety. She could already feel the effects of the drug and, coupled with the medicine for her headache, Weslee should sleep throughout the flight home.

"Yes, sir," Logan said with a laugh. "Again, I apologize for the delay."

Weslee really shouldn't have looked at him, but she couldn't help it. Their eyes met and held for several intense seconds. "I hope your urgent business wasn't bad news," she said, wondering if he'd give her an honest answer about why he'd really been delayed. Somehow she knew it had to be because of her and that utterly delicious kiss.

"No, ma'am," he said evenly. "It wasn't bad news." His penetrating blue gaze held her captive for another heartbeat before he turned and made his way to the door of the cockpit.

"Mr. Logan gets more intriguing by the minute," Inez whispered when the captain opened the door to let Logan inside.

Jon snorted a laugh. "He's too young for you, Inez." Then he peered at Weslee over his reading glasses. "As for you, young lady. He's your bodyguard. Nothing more."

"Goodness, Jon," Inez scolded, "Weslee is a grown woman. She doesn't need you giving her dating advice."

"I'm not dating him," Weslee said. "Uncle Jon is right. He is just my bodyguard." She really meant the words, but her heart wasn't listening to reason. It wanted Logan Steele. So did its owner.

"That's my girl," Jon said with a wink.

The cabin lights dimmed, shrouding Weslee from Inez's probing gaze. Feeling tired and just a tiny bit peeved with pretty much everyone, including herself, Weslee reclined her seat until it was almost flat. She didn't like feeling like this and hoped that with a good night's sleep her emotions would stabilize. She couldn't think about Logan as anything more than what he was—her bodyguard.

Pushing him out of her mind, she thought about returning home to North Carolina. She needed to get on with her life. A life without her parents.

It wasn't fair. Mama was supposed to be here to help plan her wedding, and Daddy was supposed to walk her down the aisle. They were supposed to be here when Weslee had her first baby. They were supposed to grow old together and enjoy their retirement surrounded by their grandchildren. They weren't supposed to die coming home from a weekend trip to the beach.

Tears stung the backs of her eyes. She squeezed her eyelids tight, not wanting to end this day with a crying session. Things would look brighter tomorrow morning, just like her daddy always told her. She also needed to give herself a little grace. Coming to San Diego had been her first step back into the world without the numbness of her grief. On top of that, she had a weird stalker who may or may not wish to harm her, a company to run, and the responsibility of contributing to the many charities Ground Zero supported.

The list could go on and on. Of course, she was emotionally drained.

Basically, this was life. Crazy, messy and beautiful. She could embrace it and grow stronger or wallow in self-pity until she withered away to nothing. She chose to embrace it. Suddenly, going back to the house on Emerald Isle didn't feel depressing or scary. She was lucky, really, that she had a place to go that was wrapped up with so many good memories. The thought of sharing the house with Logan when he really didn't want to be there with her hurt more.

As she drifted off to sleep, she realized she owed Logan an apology…another one, since she hadn't issued the first one. It wasn't his fault she liked him. Her hormones needed to claim that one. Dax's email had messed with her, making her vulnerable to a guy who was getting paid a lot of money to protect her and play the role of her boyfriend if the situation called for it. The kiss had been provoked by her wanting to prove they were a couple. It didn't mean anything. Even if it did, technically, Logan was the rebound guy. Everyone knew that kind of relationship was doomed from the start.

The medications she'd taken finally kicked in, allowing her to fall asleep. The next thing she knew she was trying to wake up from a bad dream. Her eyes felt heavy like she hadn't slept at all. She struggled to wake up as vague images of her dreams about dancing with Dallin Morrison, scarecrows with big boobs, helicopters, running from an unknown stalker, and being in Logan's arms surfaced. Like most dreams, they were chaotic and didn't make much sense. But the dream about being in Logan's arms had been so real.

He'd been carrying her, but she couldn't remember where they were or when he set her down. She just remembered the feel of his muscled chest, the tangy scent of his soap and the tender way he'd reassured her she was just having a bad dream.

Another fuzzy memory surfaced, and she could almost swear he'd kissed her on the forehead, which was totally ridiculous.

Hoping they'd already landed in North Carolina, she managed to force her eyes open, feeling groggy and in desperate need of the bathroom. The medication had never left her feeling like this. Of course, she hadn't ever taken the migraine medication and her motion sickness meds at the same time before. They were safe to take together but coupled with the time difference and stressful past few days, it had knocked her out cold.

Sunlight filtered through plantation shutters, which made no sense at all. Daddy's jet was nice, but it didn't have fancy shutters covering the windows. Either Weslee was still dreaming or she was in her room at the beach house.

The urge to visit the bathroom prompted her to get up. Swinging her legs down, she quickly discovered where she was as she stubbed her toe on the nightstand, knocking the lamp over. It crashed to the floor and landed on top of her already throbbing toe. Hobbling to the bathroom, Weslee finally accepted this wasn't a dream. She was fully awake and in the house on Emerald Isle.

While she washed her hands, she stared at her reflection in the mirror. She looked horrible. Black smudges underneath her bottom lashes made her eyes look puffy. Turning the water off, she leaned in to get a closer look. The puffy eyes weren't an illusion.

Hoping a shower would help, she went back into her room. Her toe must not be broken because the pain had already begun to diminish. After righting the lamp back onto the nightstand, she looked around to see if her suitcase had been brought in. If not, she still had clothing here she could wear, most likely washed and put away by her sweet mother. To her surprise, thinking about her mama straightening up her room didn't make her sad. If anything, she felt closer to her mother simply by being in the room they'd decorated together. Yellow was Weslee's favorite color. It reminded her of sunshine and happiness. Most every piece of décor in this room had been picked out on one of the many shopping trips she and her mother had taken together.

Peace washed over her as she crossed the room to open the shutters, letting more sunlight into the room. The view of the ocean from her third-story bedroom was beautiful. Memories of spending time with her parents here flooded her mind. Playing in the ocean with her daddy, hunting for washed up treasures with her mother, and taking long walks along the shoreline as a family.

A desire to create new memories with a family of her own stirred inside her. She didn't mean to let her thoughts go there, but it did anyway. She knew who she wanted to create a family with and at the same time realized that it wasn't likely to happen.

Logan had been playing a part last night. That kiss had meant nothing to him. He was her bodyguard, and she was the client.

Weslee repeated this over and over as she found her suitcase by the closet and put it on top of her bed to unpack. As she sorted through the contents of her luggage, she realized it didn't matter how many times she repeated the mantra. Her heart still wanted Logan Steele. Trying to dispute that fact was giving her another headache.

A knock sounded on the door before she could take a shower. "Weslee?" Inez called out. "Are you awake, sweetie?"

"Yes, ma'am." She patted her cheeks to give them a little color and then opened her bedroom door. Her former nanny's eyes popped open at the sight of her. "I know I look bad."

"Not too bad, especially after that nightmare you had."

"What nightmare?" Weslee asked.

Inez's forehead wrinkled with concern. "You don't remember screaming out?"

"No." She massaged the side of her head with her fingertips. "I don't remember much of anything once the medicine kicked in." She stopped rubbing her temple and frowned. "By the way, how did I get in my room?" She didn't even recall the plane landing.

A smile crinkled the skin around Inez's eyes. "Mr. Logan carried you."

Goosebumps pebbled Weslee's skin as the realization that her dream of him carrying her hadn't been a dream at all. The longing she'd felt for him was back again, only stronger. "He carried me from where?"

"The plane to the car and then from the car to your room." Inez pulled her phone from her apron pocket and tapped on the screen. "It was so sweet, and I couldn't help myself and took a few pictures of him."

An internal battle waged inside Weslee's head. One part of her shouted for her to back away and never look at the pictures, while the other part begged her to look at them, transfer them to her phone, and then have them printed to hang on her wall.

She held out the phone for Weslee to see. "I don't care what Jon says. The two of you make such a cute couple."

"We're not a couple." Weslee refused to look at the phone, telling herself that if she looked at the images they'd be forever imprinted on her mind. The dream was hazy and would eventually fade. Seeing the pictures would solidify it had happened and make it real.

She must want to torture herself for the rest of her life. Without consciously making a decision, she wrapped her trembling fingers around the phone and viewed the first picture.

Oh. My. Goodness. Why did she have to look? Logan held her in his arms like she weighed nothing. The gray dry-fit shirt he wore barely contained his bulging biceps as he confidently carried her down the stairs of the plane. Weslee tapped on the screen repeatedly, each shot making her body feel lighter and lighter until she was sure she would float away. Inez had shot more than a few pics. It was as if she'd captured every movement so if you played them in succession it would create a movie.

The closer Logan got to Inez's proximity, the more details Weslee picked up on. She might have slept through the whole thing, but that hadn't stopped her arms from circling his neck, or from snuggling in close to his chest. She paused on the next photo, studying the amused look on Logan's face as he gazed down at her.

She prayed she hadn't talked in her sleep. She'd been known to do that before, and she wasn't the kind of sleep-talker that mumbled nonsensical words. Once, she'd had a whole conversation with her mama, divulging the name of a boy she'd kissed at a party the night before. Weslee was close to her mother, but at the age of fifteen, she would've never intentionally confessed she'd kissed a boy.

That was the last picture. Before she lost her head and started scrolling backward, she handed the phone back to Inez. "You should probably delete those."

"Why would I do that?"

"Because it's embarrassing." She placed a hand over her stomach, trying to quell the butterflies knocking around inside. "Does Logan know you took those pictures?"

"If he does, he didn't say anything to me." Inez gazed down at the last picture visible on the screen once more. "I think this one is my favorite. If y'all get married we can have it printed and display it at the reception."

"Inez!" Weslee said in a voice louder than was necessary. She gently cleared her throat and softened her tone. "Please, stop saying things like that. He's just my bodyguard."

"Are you tellin' me you don't like him?" Inez shook her finger at her. "And don't you dare fib to me. I've known you since before you said your first word, and I'll know a lie if I hear it."

"No." Weslee licked her lips, knowing she had to tread very carefully. "I like him...as my bodyguard."

"I know you like him as your bodyguard," Inez said with a dramatic eye roll. "But what about as a man? Like a man you could fall in love with?"

Dropping her eyes to look at her bare feet, Weslee thought about how to reply. Inez would drag the truth out of her one way or another. So perhaps if she gave her just enough information then she would leave it alone. She couldn't tell her former nanny that she'd kissed him and might already be half in love with him, which seemed absolutely insane. But then hadn't her parents fallen in love the first time they met? Then they'd married three weeks after their first date and had just celebrated their forty-fourth wedding anniversary the month before they died.

"I like him as a man too, but that doesn't mean you can start planning a wedding." She raised her chin and lifted one shoulder up in a shrug. "Besides, just because I like him doesn't mean he likes me back."

"He likes you, darlin'." Inez pumped her eyebrows up and down. "I know a smitten man when I see one, and he is definitely smitten."

The smitten man suddenly appeared down the hall and started walking toward them. Weslee couldn't let him see her like this. She pulled Inez into her room and slammed the door shut. Turning around, she leaned against the door and closed her eyes. Hopefully, Logan would take a hint and leave her alone.

"What has gotten into you?" Inez asked.

"Nothing...I just wanted to show you my toe." She kept her voice to a whisper and held out her foot. The toe hardly looked red at all. "The lamp fell on it. I thought it was broken."

"Are you sure it didn't hit your head?" Inez asked dryly.

Another knock sounded at the door. Weslee stifled a yelp and put her finger up to her lips. "Shhh," she whispered, hoping the older woman would just go along with this.

Inez let out a huff and shook her head, muttering a prayer to the Lord for more patience.

Another knock sounded at the door. "I already know you're awake," Logan said in his deep voice. "And I know you're dressed, so I could walk right in."

Weslee reached behind her and locked the door.

He snorted a laugh. "You seriously think that is going to stop me?"

"No, but it'll at least deter you," she called back. Then she pointed a finger to her face. "I look horrible," she whispered to Inez. "I don't want him to see me like this."

Inez snapped to attention. "Go get in the shower and I'll take care of this." She motioned for Weslee to come away from the door and then pushed her toward the bathroom. "Take all the time you need."

Weslee hurried back to her bathroom and closed the door. She snickered when she heard Logan's exasperated voice. "I really need to talk to her."

"You can talk to her once she's out of the shower."

"Right, and then she'll need to fix her hair and put on makeup. I can't wait that long."

Weslee couldn't help hoping he couldn't wait that long because he wanted to kiss her again. *No, you are not to think about that kiss again.* She hoped if she told herself this over and over eventually she'd actually listen.

"What's so important that you need to see her right now?"

"I need access to her computer, but the password Jon told me to use doesn't work."

Weslee covered her mouth so she didn't groan out loud. She'd been prompted to change her password the week before and had put in the first thing that popped into her head. It had been right after she'd run into Logan when she didn't know he was Logan. She'd planned on changing it, but had forgotten to do it until now.

"Let me get it from her," Inez said. She knocked on the bathroom door. "Weslee, Logan needs your new password for your laptop."

Beads of sweat broke out across her forehead. What should she do? She could hurry and turn on the shower and hope they'd think she hadn't heard them talking. No matter what, she couldn't reveal her password with Logan standing right there.

Tiptoeing across the floor, she turned the water on and winced when it made a loud squealy noise.

"Weslee? Did you hear me?" Inez asked through the door.

"No." She slapped a hand over her mouth and then realized it was too late for that. "I'm getting in the shower. I'll talk to you when I get out."

There was silence, so she quickly stripped out of her pajamas. It occurred to her that once she was in her room someone had helped her undress and then put on her PJs. Surely Inez wouldn't have let Logan do it. No matter how determined her nanny was that Logan was the one for Weslee, she would never resort to such unladylike tactics.

She stepped in the shower and screamed loudly as icy cold water sprayed over her. With another squeal, she moved out of the line of fire so she could adjust the temperature. Suddenly, the bathroom door flew open, forcing Weslee to move closer to the faucet so she was hidden by the tiled wall. She screamed again. The water was still ice cold, and a Navy SEAL had just busted down her bathroom door.

"Don't come any closer!" she yelled out, fumbling with the handle to get hot water. "I'm…nak…not decent."

"Why did you scream then?" Logan demanded. "You scared the sh—." He stopped mid-sentence and then finished with, "Was someone else in here?"

Finally, the water turned warm and she could think again. "No, the water was freezing." Then she peeked her head around the tile and scowled at him. "And the only person in here other than me is you, so please get out of my bathroom."

Even with the shower on, she could hear Inez laughing from her bedroom. If any other man had just barged into her bathroom while she was showering, her nanny would have killed him first and then asked questions.

Logan looked like he was going to argue with her, maybe even press her for the password. She would rather risk exposure than reveal what it was. "Please leave, Lieutenant Steele. And close the door behind you."

That prompted him to look at the door, which was splintered around the doorknob. "Sorry about that. I promise I'll fix it."

"Thank you." She risked sticking her hand out and shooed him away. "Now go, please."

As if he just realized where he was, a slow grin spread across his face, making him look every bit like the hot-boy-next-door kind of guy with a healthy dose of mischievous rogue added into the mix. She'd never been attracted to a rogue before. Heaven help her, but she was attracted to this one. Still, he needed to get out of her bathroom.

"I can shoot an arrow straight through a bulls-eye, so I'm fairly certain I could nail you dead on with a can of shaving cream," she said in her scariest voice. "You have five seconds to leave before I test my theory."

The skin around his eyes crinkled, and she could swear the man was mentally counting down. Her fingers curled around the can of shaving cream. "I'm going," he said when he had two seconds left. He grinned, then laughed out loud as he turned and finally left. When he tried to close the door it popped back open, but not quite as far. "Sorry," he called out with a snicker. "And hurry it up. I've got work to do, and I need your password."

CHAPTER 10

*L*ogan was in so much trouble. Not because he'd broken down Weslee's bathroom door or lingered longer than he'd needed to once he established her stalker wasn't hiding out in her shower. No, he was in trouble because his prediction that his life would change forever was going to come true. He'd tried getting Weslee out of his head. Tried resigning as her security detail, but Sutton wouldn't have it.

After Logan explained what had happened, the man had simply smiled and asked him if he wasn't competent enough to protect Weslee Campbell. Logan was competent. He just worried he was compromised. Then Sutton asked him if another agent would value Weslee's life more than him. Logan couldn't answer yes. He would give his life for her. Had been willing to give his life for her. Another agent might hesitate to get in the line of fire, and in those few precious seconds, she could be hurt or fatally wounded.

So, Logan hadn't quit. He was here to find the identity of the stalker and put him away so he couldn't bother Weslee anymore. Then he wanted to see if this thing with Weslee was the real deal. It went against everything he'd ever believed—that falling in love wasn't worth it because of the risk of losing them. What he hadn't understood before was that missing out on loving a woman like Weslee was far worse.

It was a little crazy how fast he'd come to that conclusion. It made him feel guilty about suggesting to the team that they cut all ties with their girlfriends before they left on their last mission. The worst had happened. Well, almost happened. They'd been captured, tortured and presumed dead, but they hadn't died.

Watching his friend, Blaine, suffer when he'd thought he'd lost Elena for good had gutted Logan. Creed had been in a similar boat, but he'd fought for Kiera and won her back.

He got why they'd been so torn up, but wasn't ready to admit his feelings to any of the guys yet. Jace still didn't know that Weslee was the same girl Logan had run into on the beach and then couldn't stop thinking about. He cared about her more than any other girl he'd ever dated. He still had reservations about the whole thing and wasn't ready to call it love, but his feelings grew stronger every moment he spent with her.

The shift had really started last night on the airplane when he'd comforted Weslee after the nightmare she'd had before landing in North Carolina. Logan had still been wrestling with everything he'd discussed with Sutton when the pilot mentioned he hoped Miss Weslee was doing okay. Apparently, she was afraid of flying, mostly on take-offs and landings. As they approached the runway in Chapel Hill, Logan had left the cockpit to check on her and found all three passengers sound asleep.

Weslee had looked so peaceful. Settling into the seat across from her, he decided to take a few minutes just to look at her. She was so incredibly beautiful. More beautiful now that he knew what a kind heart she had. Logan protected people, but Weslee nurtured them.

Since the plane was on approach, he didn't return to the cockpit. He had just closed his eyes when she'd cried out in her sleep. Logan had tried waking her up, but the medication had really knocked her out. It wasn't until he'd taken her hand that she finally calmed down. That's when he knew how much he wanted to be there for her. He wanted to wake her up from bad dreams, kiss her whenever he wanted to and find out if they had a shot at forever.

But first, he needed to find out who was sending her cryptic messages, making her protection his first priority. He rubbed his thumb along the outside ridge of the simple bracelets he'd worn for the past year, which were a reminder of his pledge to protect those who couldn't protect themselves. They had been a gift from a mother of two little Syrian girls Logan had saved when their village had been under attack.

In the midst of enemy fire, Logan had spotted the two little girls standing in the street crying and frozen in fear. Logan had Jace and Baron cover him while he dodged the spray of bullets pinging off the ground. It was like running through a massive hailstorm, trying not to get hit by one of the balls of ice. Logan had swooped in and picked up a girl in each arm and then dove for cover behind a crumbling stone wall. Both girls clung to him, no longer crying. He liked to believe it was because they felt safe, but part of him wondered if they just found comfort in knowing they wouldn't die alone.

Logan wasn't sure he or anyone else would survive. They were outnumbered and outgunned. Then three US Pave Hawks had appeared on the horizon and rescued them by dropping AGM missiles with deadly precision to silence the enemy gunfire. When it was all said and done it was a miracle there hadn't been any casualties. Plenty of civilians and soldiers had received wounds, but none of them had been mortal.

Before he and his team had shipped out, the mother of the girls had given him the two homemade bracelets to represent her two daughters, thanking him over and over in Arabic for saving their lives. Logan hadn't taken the bracelets off since then. It reminded him of why he'd become a SEAL and why he risked his life fighting for freedom for those who had never had it before.

Now they reminded him of why he would risk his life for Weslee. Only now the drive to protect her wasn't just out of duty.

Still standing outside of her bedroom, he cupped his ear against the door and heard a blow dryer. At least that meant she was out of the shower. Shaking his head, he backed away and took the stairs to the first floor where the kitchen was. Standing around wasn't going to get him the password to her computer any sooner. He couldn't wait to find out why she was being so secretive about it. According to Jon, it had never been a secret in the past. So why now?

She'd slept in this morning, so he and Jon had gone over the security of the house, property and surrounding homes. The two of them had talked with the security guards at both entrances and agreed to give Logan a list of all those admitted each day. The head of the security needed to clear it with the other residents but didn't feel like anyone would object. They all loved the Campbell family and wanted to keep Weslee safe.

Jon had given Logan the password to Weslee's laptop just before he left for a three-day legal conference in Atlanta where he was one of the keynote speakers. Logan could tell the man was hesitant to leave. Mr. Curtis had tried getting out of the obligation without success.

"I promise to guard her with my life," he'd told Jon when the car arrived to take him to the airport. That's when Jon had come right out and asked Logan about his feelings for Weslee. Logan couldn't lie and told him that he cared about her more than just his client.

He'd expected the man to react with anger, possibly fire him. Instead, he'd smiled and clamped a hand on Logan's shoulder. "I'm trusting you to take care of her." The pressure on his shoulder increased as Jon met Logan's eyes. "Don't do anything to break that trust."

He hadn't broken that trust, but he had broken down Weslee's bathroom door. In his defense, her scream had turned his blood to ice, which, ironically, was the result of an ice-cold shower. It hadn't even registered to him that she had zero clothes on at the time he'd busted the door open. It wasn't until she threatened bodily harm that he realized how compromising of a situation they were in.

It was a good thing her pseudo-uncle was gone for three days. Logan needed to have the door fixed by the time Jon returned home.

Inez pulled a fresh pan of chocolate chip cookies out of the oven just as he walked in. He inhaled the delicious scent as he took another glance at the rustic looking farm kitchen housing appliances that cost more than his truck. He knew this because one look at the elaborate stove and actual pizza oven made him look up the unfamiliar brand names online.

He sure hoped the cookies tasted as good as they smelled. If not, they'd wasted a lot of money on a fancy oven. "Are these up for grabs?" he asked Inez when she glanced over and spotted him watching her.

She glowered at him, placing her hands on her hips. "I should say no, you scoundrel."

"Scoundrel?" he asked with mock indignation. "More like a superhero. Did you see how fast I broke that door down when *we* thought Weslee was in trouble?" He emphasized the "we" on purpose. Weslee's blood-curdling scream had scared Inez just as much as it had scared him. Her face had gone so white that Logan worried she was having a heart attack.

"I suppose that is impressive." She tried not to smile but wasn't very successful. Then she sobered and shook her finger at him. "I sure hope you didn't see anything you weren't supposed to see, young man."

"Scouts honor," he said, holding up the Boy Scout sign with his fingers. "I didn't see anything." That didn't mean his imagination hadn't tried to fill in the blanks.

"Were you truly a Scout?" Inez asked, sliding the sheet of cookies onto a cooling rack.

"Yes, ma'am." He crossed the floor and took a seat at the bar. "Got my Eagle when I was fourteen."

"I'm impressed." She picked up the empty cookie sheet and stared him down. "Don't you go stealin' any of those cookies. They'll be ready to eat in five minutes."

He shook his head and pushed away from the bar. "Man, you really do think I'm a scoundrel."

"Well don't go runnin' off to pout," she said. "I'm just used to Miss Weslee snitching a few cookies when my back's turned."

Pout? Logan had never pouted in his life. He'd bet money that he hadn't even done it when he was a baby. "Oh, I'm not leaving, Miss Inez," Logan said as he rounded the bar to where a big silver bowl sat with the really good stuff in it. "And I don't even want one of your freshly baked cookies." He reached around her and grabbed a golf-ball-sized portion of cookie dough. "Not when I can have this."

"Lieutenant Steele, don't you dare eat that!" She tried to grab it from him, but Logan was taller and faster, keeping it out of her reach. She shook her finger at him again. "You'll get food poisoning."

"Never have before," he said, just before biting off half of his stolen goods.

She looked completely horrified. "I can't believe you eat raw cookie dough."

"I can't believe you don't," he said, popping the rest into his mouth.

"Don't what?" Weslee said from behind him.

It was a good thing he didn't startle easy or he would've choked on the cookie dough.

"He just ate raw cookie dough!" Inez said like he'd committed a capital crime. It didn't make sense. The woman had laughed after Logan had barged in on Weslee while she was in the shower, but was throwing a hissy fit over cookie dough?

"Why does he get to eat cookie dough when you won't ever let me?"

Now Logan felt guilty for eating the whole thing. If he'd known she wasn't allowed to eat cookie dough, then he would've shared some of his contraband with her. As good as he was at stealth ops, he didn't think he'd get close enough to the bowl to get another helping. Not with Inez standing guard over it.

"You two get out of my kitchen," she said, pushing the bowl further back on the counter. "Go work on the computer, and I'll bring you cookies and milk when they're ready."

Worry lines creased Weslee's smooth skin at the mention of the computer. "We can stay in here," she said, glancing toward the entertainment room where she kept her laptop. "I'll just run and grab my computer and be right back."

Logan couldn't imagine what a sweet girl like Weslee was hiding on her computer. Whatever it was he could easily find it, even if she deleted it. The password was harder to nail down, but that didn't matter once he had access to her files.

"I don't think so," Inez said. "If y'all stay in the kitchen then there won't be any cookies left for the barbeque this evening."

"What barbeque?" Weslee and Logan asked at the same time.

"With some of the neighbors. I told you about this, didn't I?" Inez asked, directing the question more to Logan.

"Sorry, Miss Inez, but you didn't mention anything about a barbeque." He crossed his arms over his chest. "Where is it exactly and who all will be there?" Although there hadn't been any more messages from Weslee's stalker, Logan didn't want to let his guard down.

"It will be at the Whitaker's house next door." She tore off another sheet of parchment paper for the cookie sheet pan. "I can get you a list of names, but it's just a few of the neighbors that live here year-round."

"Is Robbie going to be there?" Weslee asked, rubbing the end of her hair that hung over one shoulder.

"Who is Robbie?" Logan asked her, hoping he wasn't another one of her past boyfriends.

"Weslee's first crush," Inez answered with a smile. "He's eight or nine years older than her."

"Eleven," Weslee answered.

"Whatever," Inez said, waving her hand in front of her. "Anyway, he's recently single again…" She paused and looked at Weslee. "For the third time?"

"Um, I think it's his fourth."

"Third or fourth divorce?" Logan asked, already not liking this guy.

"Yes," the two women answered in unison.

"He's been divorced four times, and you still have a crush on him?" Logan knew he sounded a tad on the jealous side.

"I didn't say I still had a crush on him." Weslee narrowed her blue eyes at him. "And why would you care if I have a crush on him?"

"You just said you don't have a crush on him."

Her chin went up. "I don't."

"Good."

"What do you mean by that?" she asked with annoyance.

Logan stifled a laugh. He liked this side of her. Trying to act all angry when all it really did was make him want to kiss her again.

"Oh, for goodness sakes. Y'all are givin' me a headache," Inez said before Logan could provoke Weslee anymore. "Yes, Robbie and his son are staying with Mr. and Mrs. Whitaker, so they'll both be at the party." She glanced at Logan and slid the silver bowl close to her. "And I'll get you a guest list."

"The sooner the better," he said, eyeing the bowl of cookie dough and wishing he could distract Inez so he could grab another handful.

"Fine," Inez said, hovering over the bowl as if she knew Logan's thoughts. "Now, please go do whatever it is y'all need to do."

Weslee didn't argue further and made a beeline for the great room. Logan followed closely behind her. She picked up the laptop and backed away from him, keeping the device close to her chest. "You never said why you need access to my computer."

"I need to read past emails and see if I can find the IP address they were sent from."

"The police already did that, and they didn't find anything."

"Doesn't mean I won't." He moved a few paces closer to her. "I've told you I'm really good when it comes to computers."

"And you're so humble," she murmured, taking a few steps backward.

"You're kind of grumpy this morning," he said, taking another step closer. "Is it because I busted your door down?"

"No, I understand why that happened." She wrinkled her nose and inched back another step. "I'm sorry I screamed."

"So," he asked moving closer, "if it's not the door then why are you mad at me?"

"Who said I'm mad at you?"

"Weslee, I know when a woman's mad at me." Logan slowly closed the distance, trying to get a read on what had her so uptight. The chemistry was still there, but she was working really hard to keep him at a distance.

She moved further away until she had her back against the wall. She was trapped and still looked very kissable. Their gazes locked, and the memory of that hot kiss they'd shared the night before rushed to the forefront. Desire flickered in her eyes as if she were having the same memory. Could she be so prickly because she wanted to be kissed? Heck, she'd even talked about kissing him in her sleep when he'd carried her off the plane.

There was only one way to find out. "Should we just go ahead and kiss so we can get that out of the way?"

"I don't want to kiss you!" she said, fury flashing in those light blue eyes. She was lying. And she wasn't very good at it, either.

"I think you do."

"No. I. Do. Not." She pronounced each word slowly, like that would make it truer. But her eyes slipped down to look at his mouth twice during her four-word reply. Not very convincing, if you ask him.

"By the way, I'm glad you brought it up," she said, her eyes dipping down to his mouth once more. "I know that kiss on the dance floor was for your cover."

"*My* cover?" He'd already made it clear he wouldn't pull the boyfriend card unless there were a viable threat. A threat to her life, not their potential love life. Weslee was the one who said the two women she'd referred to as Scarecrow Girls didn't believe she was his girlfriend. He knew they didn't buy it, but he didn't care. He wasn't into what they had to offer.

But for some reason, Weslee had needed them to believe she was with him. It wasn't because she was in harm's way. No, it was because she liked him the way he liked her. As in he didn't want another man, especially Dallin Morrison or Robbie the divorced guy, talking to her or touching her. Right now, he was fighting the impulse to press her against the wall and finish the kiss he'd started the night before.

He couldn't help smiling at her, which only increased her ire. "It doesn't really matter now." She gently cleared her throat. "The important thing is that I know that kiss didn't mean anything."

Didn't mean anything? Logan's entire universe had shifted with that kiss. Besides, she sounded more like she was trying to convince herself that it didn't mean anything. Maybe he should kiss her again so she could reconsider her verdict.

The doorbell sounded before Logan could follow through with the pleasant task.

"I better get that," Weslee said, ducking around him.

"Wrong," Logan said, quickly catching up to her. "I need to be the one to open the door."

"Of course you do," she said, cutting him a sideways glance. "Am I allowed to stand next to you?"

"Behind me." He heard her make an irritating sound as he stepped in front of her and looked through the peephole. A man stood on the porch holding a bouquet of flowers. He was blonde, tan and wearing expensive looking clothes. He supposed some women would call him handsome.

As Logan pulled back from the peephole, that primal instinct to claim Weslee as his own was back in full force. *Mine.* That's all he could think as he reached out to unlock the door. While he couldn't positively ID the guy, his gut told him he was about to come face to face with Weslee's teenage crush.

CHAPTER 11

*W*eslee glowered at Logan's back as he peered through the peephole in the door. She wasn't sure why he made her feel so irritable. Maybe it was because he was right and she did want him to kiss her. Not that she would ever admit it to him.

Logan grunted a mild expletive as he unlocked the door.

"Would your mother approve of you saying that in polite company?" she asked, smacking him lightly on the back of his shoulder. It was like hitting a rock.

Giving her a derisive laugh, he answered *yes* and punctuated it with another mild curse word. "Don't get any ideas about ditching me," he said, swinging the door open.

Weslee let out a tiny gasp when she saw who had come calling. Robbie Whitaker stood there with a bouquet of flowers, looking handsome and every bit as charming as he'd always been. Hazel eyes that were more green than brown met hers, and she felt her girlhood crush swirling around her stomach. *Crush* wasn't really the right word. Maybe that's because she was old enough to know what a train wreck he was when it came to women. It was more like she was fond of Robbie.

Ignoring Logan, Robbie winked at her. "Do I get a hug, sweet thing?" He flashed her a megawatt smile with his perfectly white teeth. They were probably capped, but the effect was well worth the money, especially against his tanned skin that still showed very little wrinkles.

"Hey, Robbie, it's so good to see you." She tried moving next to Logan, but it was like running into a stone statue.

"Hey, man," Robbie said. "Could you please get out of the way? I need a hug from my girl."

"She's not your girl," Logan said evenly. "She's mine."

Weslee was too stunned by Logan's declaration to disagree with him. Robbie's eyes narrowed as some of his good-ole-boy charm quickly faded. "Your girl?" he said in disbelief. Then he looked at Weslee. "Is that right?"

She tried moistening her lips, but her mouth was too dry. How was she supposed to answer the question? Even though she was irritated with Logan, she was still completely aware of him, like her body was attuned to notice everything about him: The subtle scent of his masculine soap, the faint shadow of whiskers darkening his jaw and the way his shirt defined his muscles and his strength…strength he used to protect people. It was what he was good at. He'd told her that right after kissing her, and she needed to remember it.

"Logan, you're being rude," she said with a laugh. "This is my friend Robbie."

Logan's jaw tightened, his expression far from friendly. Weslee stood close enough to him to feel how rigid his muscles were, like a panther ready to strike his enemy. "Right," Logan said, surprising her by wrapping an arm around her waist and pulling her next to him. "You live next door with your parents and your son, right?"

"Dang, girl, what did you tell your boyfriend?" Robbie asked with a grimace. "I sound like a complete loser."

Before Logan agreed with Robbie, Weslee moved away from his side. "He also knows the reason y'all are staying with your parents is because of that monstrous house you're building a little ways down the beach." She reached out and gave Robbie a hug. She meant for it to be quick, but Robbie took advantage and held onto her. His cologne smelled good. It was the same expensive stuff he'd used ever since she'd known him. While he wasn't fat or flabby by any means, his body felt soft compared to Logan's.

"Sugar, you smell just like peaches and cream," Robbie said, giving her a tight squeeze before letting her go. "Now tell me when you had time to go and get yourself a boyfriend?" His eyes flickered to Logan. "I've been trying to get this girl to go out with me for the past month, and just when I thought she was going to say yes, she shows up with you."

Logan continued with the death stare. Thankfully, Inez saved the awkward moment. "Robbie Whitaker, is that you I hear out here causin' trouble?"

"Yes, ma'am," Robbie said, walking past Logan and Weslee to pick Inez up in a bear hug. "I hope you're still single. Miss Weslee pulled a fast one on me and brought home a boyfriend."

Looking like he was going to kill Robbie with his bare hands, Logan uttered another oath under his breath before pinning his eyes on Weslee. One of his eyebrows quirked up. "Seriously?" he mouthed.

"Stop being so rude," she mouthed back. "He's my friend."

Inez's laughter made her finally look away from her *boyfriend*. She still didn't know how to feel about that. She hoped Logan was prepared to play that role for the rest of their stay. Word around here spread quickly, and by tonight everyone on this part of the island would know Weslee Campbell had brought home a boyfriend.

"Goodness, you're still just as charming as ever," Inez said when he put her down.

"I guess these are for you," Robbie said, handing her the bouquet of flowers. "Since Weslee's boyfriend looks like he wants to murder me."

"Logan is harmless," Inez said. "He's just crazy about our Weslee girl is all."

Logan was not harmless. He looked downright lethal right now. And why in the world did Inez have to say he was crazy about her?

"Logan, huh?" Robbie said, turning to hold out his hand to him. "Nice to meet you, man."

"You too," Logan said, shaking Robbie's hand. "And I would only maim you, not murder you."

That made Robbie laugh out loud. When he pulled his hand away, he shook it out dramatically. "Dude, I think you're serious."

"I usually am," Logan said, without cracking a smile.

Weslee knew that wasn't true either. Logan could be very playful when he wanted to be.

"Y'all better behave," Inez said, looking pointedly at Logan. "We're family here. No fighting allowed." Inez squinted out the open front door. "My goodness, is that Josh?" she said, making everyone turn to look outside. "Why he's a grown man now."

Robbie's son had grown since the last time Weslee had seen him, like four or five inches. Josh stood next to a red sports car parked in the Whitaker's driveway. He was looking down at his phone and hadn't noticed them all gawking at him.

"Yep, that's my boy," Robbie said like a proud father. "He's a little on the shy side. A trait he didn't get from his old man."

Then he hollered out Josh's name. "Come on over here, son, and say hello to Miss Inez and Miss Weslee."

Josh's head shot up with surprise. The poor kid looked like he wanted to bolt. His eyes darted from his daddy to Weslee and then back again to his dad. "Grandma needs me to go pick up some stuff for the party," he said in a quiet voice.

"You have time to be polite." Robbie waved him over again. "Hurry up and say hey and then you can go."

"Yes, sir," Josh said, looking like a little boy more than he had a moment earlier.

"Hey, Josh," Weslee said as she reached out to give him a hug. "It's so nice to see you again."

"Hey, Miss Weslee," he mumbled, hugging her like he had spaghetti noodles for arms.

Inez hugged him next. Poor Josh was so uncomfortable, his face flushed red when the older woman released him after giving him a proper hug. The kitchen buzzer went off so Inez excused herself to go get the cookies out of the oven.

"Son, this here is Mr. Logan," Robbie said, pointing him out. "He's Weslee's new beau."

Josh stared at Logan for several long seconds. The poor kid was probably intimidated by him.

"Hi, Josh," Logan said, giving the boy a kind smile. "It's nice to meet you."

"Thank you, sir," Josh said, giving Logan a limp handshake. He pulled his hand away quickly and looked at Robbie. "I gotta go, Dad."

"Don't drive like I would," Robbie joked. "Especially if you're taking the Jag."

Josh rolled his eyes. "Yeah, I wouldn't want to turn out like you."

The scathing remark surprised Weslee, but Robbie just laughed and called his son another name for a smart mouth.

Then, shoving his hands in his pockets, he turned to Weslee and let out a dramatic sigh. "Any chance your boyfriend will let you go for a drive with me to see my new house?"

"I don't need his permission," Weslee said before Logan could respond. She could see he didn't find Robbie's sense of humor very funny and was very close to causing him bodily harm. A spark of hope lit Robbie's eyes, which she didn't take seriously. This was all a game to him. "But I'm afraid the answer is no. Logan and I have plans today and then we'll see you tonight."

"You know where to find me if you change your mind, sugar." He winked at her and gave Logan a salute as he breezed past him. "Y'all have a good day now."

Weslee quickly closed the front door just in case Logan decided to go after Robbie. She turned around to find him watching her, a hint of a smile playing at his mouth.

"Don't you dare say one word," she said, shaking her finger at him like Inez always did.

"Not even one?" His smile grew, carving the dimple in his cheek. "I mean, seriously, you can't expect me not to ask questions."

"Fine, you can ask, but I don't have to answer any of them." She marched past him and wasn't surprised when he followed right behind her. Her laptop lay on top of the small desk next to the French doors that led to the lower back deck and pool. She picked it up and faced him. "I told you I don't have a crush on him anymore."

"I have no idea why you had one on him in the first place," he said with a snort. "Something tells me Robbie Whitaker hasn't changed all that much over the years."

"You're right. He hasn't changed, but I have." She lifted one shoulder up in a shrug. "I have no desire to become Robbie's next conquest or his fifth wife."

Logan considered her for a long moment. "Good." He nodded his chin toward her computer. "So, are you going to tell me your password?"

It took her a second to adjust to the abrupt subject change. "No," she said, hugging it closer, "but I'll log in for you"

"What if I need access to it when you're not available, like say when you're taking a shower?"

"Then you can break down my door," she said dryly.

That made him laugh again. "Come on, why won't you tell me?" he asked, walking toward her. "Jon said you've never kept it a secret before."

"You're not Jon."

He stood in front of her and gave her another sexy smile. "No, I'm your boyfriend."

"Yeah, about that," she said, trying to ignore the way he made her heart race with nothing more than a smile. "Why did you tell Robbie you were my boyfriend? He's not my stalker."

One of his eyebrows rose up. "Maybe not the stalker we're looking for, but he's definitely on the prowl."

"So then why did you tell him we're together?" The question was out before she thought about the repercussions. Logan might be attracted to her, and he'd acted very much like a jealous boyfriend, but it didn't mean he wanted any of this to be real or that he wanted something more.

All traces of humor left his face as he reached out and removed the laptop from her hands, placing it on the desk. Then he looked at her with a simmering gaze that made her feel like she could hardly breathe.

"I want to kiss you again." His statement didn't hold a single note of teasing. "I guess I'm asking if that's something you want too?"

Weslee's knees turned to jelly, her head spinning with yet another change in the conversation. She gripped the edge of the desk to keep upright while she tried to formulate an answer. It was yes, of course. She desperately wanted him to kiss her. Knowing there was a chance her voice wouldn't work, she simply nodded her head.

Heat flared in his eyes, his lips lifting into that sexy smirk he could trademark and make millions on. Every cell in her body awakened as he slid his fingers along her neck to cup her face with his hands. Trembling with anticipation, her eyelids fluttered closed as he lowered his mouth to hers and touched her lips softly, lingering for only a moment. The kiss ended far too soon and she made a small whimper of protest when he broke the connection.

Still, he hadn't moved away and held her face gently in his hands. She opened her eyes to find him gazing at her with tenderness and an intense look that sent a low hum buzzing through her veins. She didn't want this kiss to end like their first kiss had. Deciding now was not the time to play demure, Weslee rose up on her toes and pressed her mouth to his.

Her bold move lit a fire between them. Logan threaded his fingers into her hair and took the lead, kissing her with a hunger that ignited a sweet swirl of desire in her. Delicious warmth spread through her, making her stomach feel bottomless and her brain fuzzy. Nothing had ever felt this amazing, and she never wanted him to stop.

"Oh, my goodness," Inez said with a gasp. "It's about time y'all decided to stop acting like idiots." Logan smiled against Weslee's mouth before he pulled away from her. They both turned to see Inez wipe the corner of her eyes. "I'm just gonna give y'all a few more minutes alone."

When she disappeared, Logan looked down at Weslee and grinned. "Your nanny is the strangest chaperone. She laughs when I bust down the door while you're taking a shower.

Praises me for kissing you and then gives me permission to keep on kissing you."

"What are you waiting for, then?" she asked, hoping Inez gave them at least another ten minutes.

The air rushed from her lungs at the smoldering look he gave before his mouth descended on hers in another searing kiss. His hand slipped into her hair again, and she leaned into him, fitting against him perfectly. Needing to be closer, she wrapped her arms around his waist as Logan kissed her thoroughly.

After several minutes, he slowed the kisses down. When he pressed one last lingering kiss on her mouth, she edged back to catch her breath and looked into his stormy eyes. "Wow," she said. "You're very good at that."

He gave her a crooked smile and ran his thumb under her bottom lip. "I don't think I'll make a very good boyfriend, Weslee."

Her heart nearly stopped beating at the serious tone of his voice. "Why do you say that?" she asked, struggling to keep up with his thought process.

His thumb moved to caress her cheek. "Because I haven't been a good one in the past."

She hated thinking of him having another girlfriend. Thinking of him kissing another woman like he'd just kissed her and gazing at her with so much tenderness it made her chest ache. "Okay." She drew in a shaky breath and backed away from him so he no longer touched her. If he planned on rejecting her, then she needed distance from him in order to think straight. "So, now what?"

A puzzled expression crossed his face, and he reached out to wrap a firm arm around her waist, pulling her back to him. "So, now we decide if you're willing to give me a chance to improve my record as a boyfriend."

Relief swept through her like a category three hurricane. "I think I can do that."

"Yeah?" He applied gentle pressure to her back, drawing her closer.

"Yes," she said, unable to come up with a witty comeback. The need for another kiss had short-circuited her brain. Arching into him, she slid her arms around his neck and pressed a lingering kiss to his mouth.

"So, about that password..." Logan said a few minutes later.

The fuzzy effects from his kisses vanished as quickly as he changed topics. "I'll give it to you," she said, stepping out of his embrace to grab the laptop. "Just as soon as I change it." Laughing, she took off down the hall in a dead run.

For once she'd succeeded in throwing Logan off balance. She made it to one of the bedrooms and had the door locked by the time he chased after her.

CHAPTER 12

*L*ogan closed the laptop and rolled his shoulders back. He hadn't found anything more than the police. The IP address pinged back to an area where there were too many public sources to define where the emails had originated.

Weslee had been on her phone for the past hour, working out marketing details for the contract with Total Works Gym and Spa. Trenton Williams had agreed to allow Ground Zero into several of his flagship gyms to test the market.

At least Logan didn't need to worry about Trenton putting the moves on Weslee. She had asked her assistant to oversee the implementation, which meant she didn't need to have any more face-to-face meetings with the guy. However, it also meant that she wasn't coming out to California either.

She glanced over at him and mouthed, "One minute." Then gave him a smile that made him want to cross the floor, toss her phone on the couch, and press her against the wall for another round of kissing. Inez was an awfully loose chaperone.

Logan knew that when Jon returned from his conference the kissing would have to be toned way down.

Getting to his feet, he stretched and walked over to look out the large picture window that almost took up the whole wall. From the third level of the house, he could easily see over the dunes, giving him a magnificent view of the Atlantic Ocean. Rolling waves crashed onto the shore, darkening the sand as the water stretched further with each wave.

"Sorry that took so long," Weslee said, coming up behind him and slipping her arms around his middle. "Want to go for a walk?" she asked, pressing her cheek against his back.

The second she touched him his pulse went from a nice steady rhythm all the way to full throttle. "Yeah." He covered her hands with his, knowing his feelings for Weslee had gone full throttle too. He had fallen in love with her, and it wasn't just all about the physical chemistry between them. It wasn't that she was the most beautiful woman he'd ever seen, or how sweet she was, or how generous she was with her money. It was all of that combined and something so much deeper he couldn't put words to it.

Robbie had been the catalyst Logan needed to make him see what was right in front of him. After going through her email and social media messages, the guy wasn't Weslee's only admirer. Dallin Morrison had also been messaging her, asking if he could take her out to dinner the next time he was near the East Coast. All Weslee had to do was give him the green light and the politician would be here on the next flight out.

Logan turned around so Weslee was in his arms. He didn't want to let this woman go. Ever. He couldn't guarantee nothing would happen to him or to her. No amount of strength or skills could ward off a terminal illness, but he also knew she was worth the risk.

"I could get used to this," he said, tightening his hold on her.

"Me too." She tipped her face up and studied him for a long moment, her beautiful eyes filled with love for him. The words *I love you* were on the tip of his tongue. It was so obvious that she shared his feelings. If she told him she loved him could he say it back? He'd never uttered those three little words to another woman besides his mother.

"If you keep looking at me like that, Miss Campbell, I'll be forced to take action."

Her lips parted in a sweet but very sexy smile that lured him in like a kid in a candy store. "That's what I'm counting on, sailor."

Grinning, Logan bent his head and covered her mouth with his. He was unprepared for the shockwave of emotions that rocketed through him the second their lips touched. Somehow acknowledging the depth of his feelings for her had become an accelerant, like throwing gasoline onto a fire. It consumed him as he kissed her deeply, tasting her and breathing her in.

"We better go for that walk," Logan said, forcing himself to end the kiss. Miss Inez had gone to help her neighbor prepare for the gathering that evening, so he and Weslee were completely alone. It was far too tempting to push for something more. "Come on," he said, taking her hand, "before I do something your nanny will not approve of."

They walked hand in hand down the private boardwalk that took them across the dunes and down to the beach.

"You didn't find anything on my computer, did you?" she asked.

"Nope." He intertwined their fingers together and looked at her. "Guess I'm not a hotshot computer geek after all." He almost pressed her about her password again, which she'd changed before he could unlock the door of the bedroom she'd run into with her computer. He also hadn't found anything incriminating in her files. He would get that password out of her, eventually.

"Guess you're not," she said with a laugh, slipping off her shoes before they left the boardwalk.

It was an overcast day with a light breeze. Weslee shivered when her bare feet hit the sand, and he saw goosebumps on her arms. "Do you want to go back and get a jacket?"

"No," she said, snuggling in close to him. "Not when I have you to keep me warm."

Chuckling, Logan let go of her hand so he could wrap his arm around her shoulders. "Better?" he asked in a rough voice. *Shoot.* He was so gone on this girl. He was going to be eating crow when his team found out. Especially Jace, who liked to refer to someone who falls in love as a single person dying.

"Much," she said, leaning her head against his bicep.

He scanned the area before they set off on their walk. Logan saw very few people out. Just a woman walking her dog and further down the beach there was a group of kids playing volleyball. The ocean roared as a large wave rolled in and crashed onto the shoreline. "Which way?" he asked.

"Let's go this way," she said, pointing in the direction of the Whitaker's house. "I'd like to see if the Rowlings are here visiting." She went on to explain how she'd mentored the two Rowling girls the year before, teaching them all about archery. She wanted to make sure they were signed up for the fundraising tournament in a few weeks.

Logan remained vigilant as they passed by the next-door neighbor's property. Although he didn't see Robbie or any other family members, he sensed they were being watched. He wished he could've pinned Robbie as the stalker, but given the frequent communication between him and Weslee and his open admiration and persistence in getting her to go out with him, he doubted the guy would also send her anonymous messages that would drive her away.

"Are you ever going to teach me to shoot an arrow?" he asked as they approached the Rowling's beach house. He'd found some of her archery equipment stored in the garage when he'd explored the house this morning. In the game room, her dad had also dedicated one of the walls in honor of all the awards she'd won over the years, including the bow and arrows she'd used to win her first championship. She was good, and he'd like to see her in action.

"I would love to," she said, giving his hand a squeeze. "But we better pick a day that isn't so windy or you'll never come close to hitting a bullseye."

"Is that a challenge?"

"If it is it wouldn't be a fair one," she said with amusement.

Logan came to a stop so he could look at her. "You're talking smack with the wrong guy."

"I'm not talking smack. I'm just letting you know that I'm good and I can almost guarantee I would win."

"Want to bet on it?" he asked.

"What are the stakes?"

He considered her for a moment. A kiss would've been his first choice, but since she liked kissing him as much as he liked kissing her it would be a moot point. "You have to tell me what the password was."

"And what do I get when I win?"

"*When?*" he asked with a low chuckle. "Your trash-talk is only making me more determined."

"Don't say I didn't warn you." She slipped her arms around his neck, her fingers playing with the hair at his neck. "So, what's my prize?"

A diamond ring? was the first thought that entered Logan's mind. Shoot, the once crazy thought didn't sound as crazy anymore, which made him want to put on the brakes. But gazing into those eyes of hers was like a runaway truck coming down a hill, gaining momentum with each passing second. He couldn't stop even if he wanted to. He wasn't even sure an emergency truck ramp would help.

"What do you want it to be?" he asked, slipping his hands to her lower back so he could pull her closer.

Now it was her turn to consider him. Logan got lost in pools of blue, knowing that whatever she asked of him he'd want to give her. "I need time to think about it," she finally said in a soft voice.

As he lowered his head, she rose up to meet his mouth. He kissed her, long and slow, wondering how he had ever lived without her. The kiss came to an end when her cell phone pinged several times in a row. "You better see if that's Miss Inez before she comes looking for us."

She sighed heavily. "I suppose you're right." She gave him a peck on the lips before releasing her hold to pull her phone from her back pocket. She swiped the screen and all the color drained from her face.

"What is it?" Logan asked moving so he could see the screen. He swore and took the phone from her. "Now he's crossed a line," he said between clenched teeth.

The picture of him and Weslee dancing at the charity ball had been edited so that a red X was painted over Logan's face. The accompanying messages had been sent in one word increments, and they were not directed at Weslee. They were meant for Logan.

Leave. Her. Alone. Or. You're. A. Dead. Man.

Feeling like he had a sniper's bead on him, he cursed himself for leaving his gun back at the house. Worse, Weslee was just as visible as he was. "Let's get back to the house," he said, not knowing if he should get in front of her or behind her to lessen her exposure. "You up for a run?" he finally settled on, taking her hand and pulling her along with him before she could make a reply.

Whoever took this picture had been at the ball, and because he'd been too busy moving in a for a kiss, he had missed him. Maybe he wasn't the best man to protect Weslee after all. At the very least, he needed backup for the archery tournament.

He knew Kate was on another detail that week, but he wasn't sure about Jace or any of the other members of his team. Once he notified Detective O'Brien about the escalated threat, he would send out a text to the guys to see who might be available.

"What do we tell Inez?" Weslee panted as they hurried across the boardwalk.

"Everything," Logan said, not sure if the same held true for Jon. He wouldn't be able to do anything more if he were here. Still, he'd ask for Weslee and Inez's input before he talked to him. "She needs to be alert."

"Okay." Then Weslee stumbled and cried out in pain. Logan hadn't let her put her shoes on and now her big toe was bleeding from where she'd stubbed it.

"Sorry," he said, sweeping her up into his arms. "This isn't going to be comfortable." He carried her over his shoulder in a fireman's carry so he didn't lose any momentum.

Once they were safely inside, he located a first-aid kit and doctored Weslee's toe. She was very quiet the entire time. When he finished, she took his hand and curled her fingers tightly around it.

"I saw that same picture on Instagram while I was on the phone today. Someone tagged me in it, so I know the post is recent."

Logan pressed the home button to bring up the screen of apps. He didn't want Weslee to dwell on the photo of him or the threatening message. "Will you please find it for me?" he asked, noting her trembling fingers as she nodded her head and took the phone.

"Here you go," she said, handing him back the phone.

"Do you know this person?" he asked, reading over the innocuous caption. @ShopTillYouDrop had noted what a cute couple they made and then asked where Weslee Campbell shopped for her date. Weslee had over two hundred thousand followers, so weeding through the thousands of comments would take time. He'd send it to AJ, his white-collared IT guy he'd brought in as a partner for his cybersecurity company.

He looked over some of the other posts she'd been tagged in. One of them was a shot of her in front of one of the cancer research children's hospitals here in San Diego. Logan recognized the dress. It was the same white dress she'd had on that day he'd run into her on the beach. He tapped on the picture and scrolled to the bottom of the comments to find the date stamped, which coincided with the day he'd first met Weslee. The caption by @CancerSurvivor was as innocent as Weslee was in all of this. "I want to grow up to be just like this amazing woman…thanks to her I'll get that chance."

"Do you know this person?" he asked, showing Weslee the picture.

She studied it for a moment. "I recognize her name, but don't know her personally." She leaned in close, her hair brushing against Logan's forearm. "That picture was posted a few hours before I met you…ran into you on the beach."

"I know." He let out a frustrated breath. Maybe her stalker hadn't been to California that day after all? If the guy was a regular follower then he would've seen this picture. The news didn't comfort him because it was going to take a lot of time trying to find someone who consistently followed every post Weslee was tagged in.

After sending a message to AJ and Detective O'Brien, Logan sent out an SOS to his team. "I need someone to cover my six in a couple of weeks...any takers?"

The replies came in one by one. If they could swing it, his guys would gladly provide backup. Now he just had to find out who wanted him dead.

CHAPTER 13

*W*eslee knew Logan wasn't very happy with her right now. She'd insisted on going to the party when all he wanted to do was lock her in her room and not let her out until he found out who had sent the message. He'd grudgingly relented after receiving a report from the guards at both checkpoints that there had been no visitors today.

The upside about all of this was Logan hadn't left her side once. The downside was Robbie had noticed and he'd had too much to drink, which was a bad combination. He wasn't a happy-go-lucky drunk either. The alcohol had the opposite effect on him. His brooding stares were increasing with every trip he made to the bar.

Josh was just as brooding, but it was all directed at his father. He had only made eye contact with Weslee and Logan once, and that had been when they'd first arrived at the house.

"Someone needs to cut that guy off," Logan said. "He's so loaded he can hardly stand up straight."

"At least he won't be driving home tonight."

"Yeah, but he could still go out somewhere." Logan put a

protective hand to her lower back. Warmth spread through her as she leaned in close to him. He'd touched her frequently tonight like he needed the connection to assure him of her safety. She loved how protected she felt and couldn't help thinking how much her parents would've liked Logan. "I don't like the way he's looking at you either," he said in a menacing voice.

"I think those looks are more for you," she said, cutting a sidewise glance to Robbie. He was working on another drink, glaring at either her or Logan. She couldn't decide. "Or maybe not." She rubbed her lips together. "But Robbie would never hurt me."

At least she hoped that was the case. A memory of him a few years earlier surfaced. He'd been married at the time, but like tonight, he'd had too much to drink. He'd been waiting for her when she'd come out of the bathroom and cornered her in the darkened hallway. She still had a crush on him back then, so having him pay attention to her had been conflicting until he'd confided in her that his marriage was over and that he was just waiting for the papers to be filed. Weslee hadn't seen his wife all evening, making her believe his claim.

Robbie had told her how much he missed seeing her and suggested they find an empty bedroom to get reacquainted. He hadn't been drunk enough to miss the shocked look on her face. "We won't do anything you don't want to do," he'd said, reaching out to finger a strand of her hair. "But I've been fantasizing about running my fingers through your hair all night long, among other things." Then he'd moved in to kiss her. Weslee had been frozen. She'd wanted Robbie for so long, but she'd learned a long time ago to never take anyone drunk seriously.

Before his lips touched hers, she'd ducked under his arm and told him to call her when the divorce was final and he was sober. He never had contacted her. It wasn't until the following year that she'd seen him again. By then he had a new wife.

An uneasy feeling came over her at the memory. Robbie had liked her hair. Now that she thought about it, he had always liked her long hair. But he couldn't be the one stalking her. They had been openly communicating for the past month. The messages from her stalker had started at least two weeks earlier and had been emailed to her. The texting didn't start until a couple of weeks ago, forcing her to change her phone number. She'd only given the new number to those in her contacts but that was still a lot of people.

"Drunks should never be trusted," Logan said in an even voice.

Weslee's stomach felt hollow. Should she tell Logan about her memory? She glanced at Robbie. He wasn't looking at her anymore. He was all smiles and talking to a leggy blonde she didn't recognize.

Her relief that Robbie had a date was short-lived when the pretty girl waved goodbye to him and then went over to Josh, kissing him on the mouth as a greeting. Josh's response was way off for a guy who had just been kissed by a beautiful girl. He'd broken the kiss off and then led the girl over to the bar. Although he wasn't old enough to be drinking, nobody seemed to care when he ordered him and his girlfriend a drink and then disappeared inside the house.

"Besides, we should go soon," Logan whispered in her ear. "I don't think that storm is going to miss us like the weatherman predicted."

"That's what Inez thinks too." Weslee glanced at her watch. "We've been here for an acceptable amount of time. Let's go find her to see if she's ready to go home."

It took a few minutes to work their way through the crowd to where Inez sat with Mrs. Whitaker and two other women

Weslee didn't know that well. From the corner of her eye, she noticed Robbie tracking her again. She should've never encouraged him by responding to his texts. Now that she thought about it she had been sort of flirting with him even though she had no intention of getting tangled up with him.

"I was just going to come find y'all," Inez said, scooting back from the table. "That storms movin' in and I'd like to fill all the bathtubs up with water just in case the power goes out."

"That's a good idea," Mrs. Whitaker said. "I think we should probably call it a night so y'all can get home safely."

"Why do they want to fill their bathtubs with water?" Logan whispered in Weslee's ear. His warm breath sent a shiver of pleasure all the way down to her toes.

"In case the water gets shut off." Weslee smiled at the confused look on his face. "Inez is old school and forgets we have a basement stocked with cases of bottled water. It's just something she's always done."

The party guests were all too familiar with how wicked a storm could get and how fast it could change, so everyone quickly helped clean up, taking the dishes inside. Before heading home, Weslee went to the bathroom. It was the same one she always used when visiting, and just like before, Robbie stood outside waiting for her when she came out.

"It's about time I got you all to myself," he said, his voice not nearly as slurred as she'd expected. "Your boyfriend is too possessive. He's the type that stalks you when the relationship ends."

His use of the word *stalk* gave her that uneasy feeling again. "Who says the relationship is going to end?"

"They always do." He grinned. "Trust me, I'm an expert by now. I can't tell you how many women have continued to harass me after I've ended things." He looked her over, his eyes lingering on her chest. Her shirt wasn't low cut, but it did fit her snuggly. "You're so beautiful." He stared at her with a hungry look that frightened her. "You have no idea how much I want you right now."

"Robbie, you're drunk." She saw Logan coming her way. "Go sleep it off before someone gets hurt."

"Hey," Logan said. "What's going on?"

Robbie backed out of the way. "Nothing, dude," he said, holding his hands up like he was innocent. "Just telling Weslee how pretty she looks tonight."

"Is that right?" Logan asked her.

Weslee didn't want a fight to break out...or for Robbie to get beat up. Since Robbie had told her how beautiful she was, she decided to stick with that. "Yes." She took Logan's hand. "Have a good night, Robbie."

"Me and a bottle of Jack Daniels plan to," he said with a derisive laugh.

"Has he had a drinking problem before?" Logan asked as he led her to the back door where Inez waited for them.

"He's not an alcoholic that I know of." She wasn't sure though. This was the south and here folks tended to sweep things like that under the rug, so to speak. "Inez has never said anything about it so I think Robbie is just having a bad night."

"Did he say anything else to you besides how beautiful you are?" Logan asked before they reached the back door. "I want all of the truth."

She couldn't outright lie to him. Not if she hoped to have a long-term relationship with him. "Will you promise me you won't do anything to embarrass the Whitakers?"

Logan muttered another curse word. "What did he say to you?" he growled.

"Promise me, Logan." She glanced at Inez who was hugging the neighbor's goodbye. "Please."

"All right. I promise," he bit out. His eyes blazed with anger, but it wasn't directed at her.

She told him what Robbie had said, grateful she hadn't divulged the things Robbie had said to her all those years ago. Every line in Logan's face was tense, making his boyishly charming face look like granite. But he kept his promise. Other than the tightening of his jaw and clenching his fists, he didn't say one thing. Not even a muttered curse word.

"It's so nice to meet you, young man," Mrs. Whitaker said, giving Logan a hug. That was another thing about the south. They were all huggers. "Inez can't say enough nice things about you."

"Thank you, ma'am." He smiled at Inez. "Miss Inez knows how much I love her and her cookie dough."

That earned him a swat on the arm from Weslee's mild-mannered nanny. "This one is trouble," Inez said with a laugh. "It's a good thing I like him enough to want to keep him forever." She leaned in and whispered loud enough for everyone to hear. "I meant for Weslee to keep him forever."

Weslee was embarrassed and didn't want to look at Logan. Another southern trait was no filter, especially with the older generation.

"My goodness, Miss Weslee, it sounds like you've found yourself a keeper."

Weslee was so relieved that Mrs. Whitaker had said *keeper* instead of *husband* that she didn't try to dispute her words. "Yes, ma'am. He's a good man."

She could feel Logan's eyes on her but she only dared to look at him when he opened the door for Inez to pass through first. His eyes smoldered—that's the only way to describe it—with something she couldn't define. But the look sent a bolt of lightning through her that heated every square inch of her body.

As they stepped outside, Weslee caught sight of Josh walking toward the ocean. He turned and stared at her for a brief moment. She started to lift her hand to wave at him, but he abruptly turned and continued toward the water. She felt sorry for him. It was clear that Robbie was more of a buddy to his son than a father figure. Since the young man was alone, she figured his girlfriend must have left.

A gust of wind whipped at her hair. The air was thick with humidity and had a chill to it that ordinarily would have left her freezing. Having Logan holding her hand and remembering the heated look in his eyes made it feel like she stood in front of a roaring fire.

Once they were inside, Inez hurried to fill up all the bathtubs with water on the main floor. She instructed Weslee and Logan to do the same on the other floors while she gathered flashlights in case the generator didn't work properly.

"I'm sleeping on the couch upstairs," Logan said as they made it to the first bathroom.

"There's another bedroom you can take," Weslee said. "It's more comfortable than the couch."

She expected him to argue with her but he remained quiet, staring at her with a pensive gaze. "I don't know how good of a man I am." The grave sound of his voice countered how off-balance his statement made her feel. "I've done things and seen things that would make you run right into Dallin Morrison's arms and never look back."

Okay, she was starting to get used to his out-of-the-blue statements, but this one puzzled her and ticked her off too. "I don't want to run into his arms, Logan."

She didn't like the hard lines on his face, making him look like a warrior on a mission. She liked the sexy spy or hot-guy-next-door so much better, but she supposed if she loved him she would have to love all of him.

Love. She did love him—so much that it physically hurt to think he might not return her feelings. "It's your arms I want to run into." She licked her lips, yearning to tell him she'd fallen in love with him. "And you can't chase me away. Not when everything you've done was done as a SEAL." She lifted her hand and smoothed the lines on his forehead with her fingertips. "I can't imagine the things the Navy required you to do or the lives that were lost, but have you ever stopped to consider all the lives you did save? How many women and children are alive because of you?" She dropped her hand to her side. "You've told me over and over that you protect people. And, the thing is, Logan, I believed you the first time you told me that the day on the beach when I ran into you. I still believe in you."

His eyes burned into hers like he was trying to trust what she was saying was true. Then he looked down at the two thin bracelets he wore, rubbing his thumb across the ridge of one of them. The silence stretched, but she kept quiet even though she desperately wanted to ask him about what those bracelets meant to him.

"A Syrian woman…a mother gave these to me after I rescued her two daughters." He moved his thumb to the second bracelet and let out a shaky breath. "Two little girls were standing in the middle of the street, crying and frozen in fear as bullets sprayed over and around them. I couldn't leave them there to die like that. I had some of my team cover my six while I rushed out to grab them."

He raised his face to look at her. "I didn't think we'd make it out alive. I knew it was a miracle when I dove behind a wall and all three of us were alive without one single bullet wound."

The love she felt for this man swelled inside her. He did protect people. She sensed he protected his heart too. What would it take for him to trust her enough to give her his heart?

"I can't imagine having that much courage to run into the line of fire to save people I didn't know, but you did." She wanted to reach for him but wasn't sure if he'd welcome her touch again. "I'm sure the girls' mother felt so helpless, not knowing how to save her little girls. And then a brave American soldier swooped in and saved her daughters for her. You did that, Logan. Those girls are alive because of you. They have a future because of you."

His eyes softened, and the tension drained from his expression. "Thank you." Maintaining eye contact, he reached for her hand and brought it to his mouth, placing a heated kiss to her palm. "I'm not good enough for you," he said, still holding her gaze as if he wanted to gage her true reaction. She hoped he read how much she loved him. "But I want to try to be, Weslee." He kissed her palm again. Then he reeled her into him and placed a lingering kiss to her mouth, bathing her in warmth, security, and love.

A sense of well-being settled over her that everything would work out. Yes, he hadn't declared his love for her, but he hadn't pushed her away. She loved him and she would tell him. She just needed the right moment to do it.

CHAPTER 14

*T*he wind howled outside as a torrent of rain pelted the large glass windows. Logan couldn't sleep with this raging storm going on, even if thinking about Weslee had already robbed him of sleep. The couch was comfortable enough, just not long enough. Swinging his feet around, he sat up on the couch and scrubbed his hands over his face.

He was not falling in love with Weslee. He'd already done it. The love he felt for her filled up every empty space inside of him. It soothed fears he'd had his whole life. It healed wounds he'd gotten each time he went out on a mission and took another life to save countless other lives.

It still blew his mind that she thought he was a good man. It reminded him of when Sutton had shown up in Turkey to recruit Logan and his SEAL team to take part in his Warrior project. He'd called all of them heroes. They hadn't felt like heroes. They were just doing what they'd been trained to do, but then Sutton had pointed out each thing they'd done that was more than just part of the job. He'd looked Logan in the eyes and called him a hero for having the guts to fly a chopper when he'd never done it before. Some would call it stupid. If the guy knew anything about him then he'd know that was just Logan winging it again. Still, the words had stayed with him.

Weslee had called him courageous. So why did he feel like he wanted to bolt one minute and then beg her to marry him the next? It wasn't fair to her. He needed to let go of his fears—he was man enough to admit they were fears—and be all in. Or he needed to let her go.

That thought made his gut twist into so many knots no sailor would ever untangle them. He didn't want to let her go. He needed to draw on that bravery because he was finding out that it took a lot of courage to love someone. Even more so to allow yourself to be loved. He hadn't been a ruthless killer or a warlord. He hadn't done any of it for power or for money. He'd done it out of a sense of duty to protect the innocent and maintain freedom.

So, could he believe what Weslee had said to him? That he was a good man?

A sudden gust of wind battered the window. He half-expected it to shatter. Maybe he should've insisted they use the hurricane shutters. It wasn't too late to close them. They were electronic and Weslee had shown him where the control panel was earlier. He got up from the couch and navigated around the furniture to turn on a light. It was so dark and without wearing night vision goggles he couldn't see much.

Flipping the switch on, he squinted against the light and hurried down the hall to where the panel was. As he opened the door, another burst of wind rattled the house. The lights flickered on and off several times. He pressed the button to close the shutters when a surge of wind shook the house so much he could feel it inside him. Then everything went dark and so quiet. The underlying hum of electricity he hadn't noticed before no longer filled the air.

"Logan?" Weslee called out to him. She stood next to the empty couch, holding a small LED lantern.

"I'm here," he said. She swiveled in his direction, the small lantern lighting a path toward her. "Thought I might close the shutters, but I waited too long."

Walking toward him, she met him near the small kitchenette. The lantern created enough light for him to see how cute she was with her hair messed up. Dang, it was sexy too. He swallowed hard, not letting his mind go where it shouldn't be going. Inez had lectured him soundly when she found out he was sleeping on the couch near Weslee's bedroom. She'd told him that she liked him, but not so much that she wouldn't hesitate to shoot him if he comprised her girl.

Kissing...that was allowed, but his hands couldn't go exploring. She'd said a bunch of other stuff that had him feeling like a hormonal teenager without any self-control. Logan promised her he wouldn't violate her rules. He never broke a promise he could control, and he knew how to control himself. Discipline had been ingrained in him from as far back as he could remember.

His eyes skimmed over her yellow pajamas. They weren't revealing and could probably pass for a T-shirt with matching shorts. The simplicity of the clothing was more appealing because she looked incredibly kissable. Desire swamped his senses, his body reacting to her nearness and making his brain foggy.

One kiss. That's all he wanted was one kiss. But with her looking all sexy like that he knew one kiss wouldn't be enough. He was still a man. A good man, according to Weslee. He wanted her to keep that opinion of him. That, and he didn't want to get shot by a sixty-something former nanny.

"Which side of the house is the generator on?" he asked, knowing it should've automatically kicked on by now.

A wrinkle creased her brow. "On the north side but the panel is inside the garage. I wonder why it didn't come on? It should've started working soon after the power went out."

"Why don't you go back to bed and I'll go check it out," he said, already knowing she would tell him no by the stubborn look on her face.

"I'm coming with you." The windows shook again, prompting her to move closer to him. "Inez took her sleeping pill. She wouldn't wake up if a freight train came through her bedroom." She jumped when debris hit the window. "I don't want to be up here alone."

That ingrained protectiveness inside of him doused his physical desires for now. "Sure, I could probably use your help." He took her hand and led her back to the couch. "Let me get grab my flashlight."

He found it on the end table next to the couch, along with his watch. His gun was there too, but it was in a small gun safe he could open quickly with his fingerprint. He grabbed the flashlight and they headed down the stairs.

"This storm is nothing compared to a real hurricane," Weslee said when the house shook from another gust of wind.

"Then I hope I never witness a real hurricane." He shone the flashlight on the second-story windows. "This storm puts a Colorado blizzard to shame."

As they made their way to the main level, she asked him how many blizzards he'd been in. He found himself telling her about the time he'd walked a half mile to school in a snowstorm that would've canceled school if it had been anywhere else but Colorado. It was right before his dad had died. He was only nine and had told his mom that he needed to get used to doing hard things if he wanted to be a SEAL.

He'd bundled up in his winter gear and walked to school. At the time, he hadn't known his mom had followed him at a discreet distance to make sure he'd arrived safely. He'd only learned about it on his first deployment. She'd hugged him tight and told him she wished she could follow him in her car to make sure he was safe. Logan had vowed to do whatever it took to return to his mom. She'd already suffered enough when his dad had been killed.

He told Weslee all of that too, which he hadn't planned on doing. She stopped walking, set her lantern on top of a sofa table, and turned to look at him. The shimmering light of lantern illuminated her beautiful face perfectly. She was crying. He hadn't meant to make her cry.

"That is the sweetest thing I've ever heard," she said, wiping a tear with the tip of her finger. Another one escaped and slid down her smooth skin before she could wipe it away. "Your mother sounds wonderful. No wonder you turned out so amazing."

Her praise made him feel uncomfortable. He'd been a good kid with good grades, but there were times he'd probably given his mom some of her gray hair. "I was still a pain in the..." He paused to reword how much of a pain he was. "...behind."

"You mean you weren't perfect?" She was teasing him, and he couldn't resist kissing her this time. He set his flashlight next to the lantern and pulled her into his arms.

Like oxygen fanning a flame back to life, kissing Weslee stoked a fire inside Logan until he was close to breaking his promise to Inez. He quickly pulled his hand away from Weslee's waist. Without willfully thinking about it, his hand had inched up until his palm connected with her warm skin.

"You're going to get me shot by your nanny," he said, stepping away from her so he could think straight again.

"Inez threatened to shoot you?" She touched a finger to her lips. "For kissing me?"

Heat simmered low in his belly as he considered her plump lips. "Kissing is allowed." He ran a hand through his hair. "It's the other stuff she said she'd shoot me for."

"Oh." Weslee bit her lower lip, trying to hide her smile. "Well, I don't want her to shoot the man I love." Her eyes widened, and she slapped her hand over her mouth.

She loved him? He'd heard that correctly, right?

"I didn't mean to say that out loud," she said, apologizing before he could confirm what he'd heard. "At least not yet." She pushed a section of her long hair behind her ear. "I was waiting for the right moment to tell you."

Logan was rendered speechless. This beautiful girl loved him. Loved *him*, even after he'd told her he wasn't good enough for her. His mind scrambled for what to say. His mouth felt like it was stuffed with cotton. "I…" He wanted to tell her he loved her too, but the words stuck in his throat.

She searched his face, and he saw her hope dwindling. "You don't need to say anything, Logan." She lifted one shoulder up in a shrug. "But now you know how I feel about you."

Come on, Steele. Pull it together. "It's not that I don't—" He stopped and drew in a breath. He was botching this whole thing. He hoped she'd cut him some slack. He wasn't the romantic type, and he'd never done this before. Never thought he would.

Logan saw a shadow and went on alert, but it was too late. As if in slow motion, he watched in horror as a man grabbed Weslee around the waist and yanked her to him. Then the man pointed a gun at her head. "Don't make a move or she's dead."

Red-hot rage rivaled with his fear of losing Weslee as Logan stared into the cold face of Josh Whitaker. The kid was Weslee's stalker? Carefully, Logan held up his hands.

"I said don't move!" Josh shouted, pressing the gun into the side of Weslee's head. She winced as terror flickered across her face.

"Okay, man," Logan said. "I just want to show you I'm unarmed." He couldn't believe he'd left his gun upstairs or that the kid got in past the security system. Then he remembered the power was out and the whole-house generator hadn't kicked on. Josh must have somehow disabled it. "I know you don't want to hurt Miss Weslee," he said, keeping his voice even. "So let's talk about what's going on. I'd like to help."

"You can't help me!" Josh yelled, spittle spraying from his mouth. "Because of you my plan is ruined."

Logan wished like heck Blayze Brockton, another former SEAL working for Sutton, was here for backup as a hostage negotiator. Now he wished he'd asked his guys to come as soon as possible. He was still waiting to hear back from them on final dates for all of Weslee's upcoming events.

Clearing his mind of things he couldn't control, he concentrated on what he could do. He needed to keep the kid talking until he could figure out a way to disarm him. "I'm sorry." He needed to know whatever plan he'd screwed up if he had any hope of saving Weslee. "What can I do?"

Josh let out a string of curse words and pointed the gun at Logan. He instantly felt better because he was the target and not Weslee. The kid's hand shook violently, giving him hope that he would lose his grip on the gun.

"You can die," Josh seethed "I need you gone so my dad can hook up with Weslee."

What? This was all about Robbie getting together with Weslee? Logan swallowed, trying to understand the kid's twisted thoughts.

Before he could think of what to say, Josh filled in a few more blanks. "Then I can pay him back for what he did to me."

Whoa, this whole mess just got messier. The kid had daddy issues. Anyone would with Robbie as a father. "I get that. My old man makes me mad too." He knew his father would forgive the lie if he was still alive, but Logan needed to find some commonality with Josh.

"Yeah? Did he sleep with your girlfriend too?"

Weslee gasped, and Josh jerked the gun back at her, making Logan's blood turn to ice. This was so messed up. Never mind that a father would actually sleep with his son's girlfriend, but Josh's revenge plan was to rape Weslee because he knew she'd never have consensual sex with him.

He needed to humanize Weslee otherwise the kid might pull the trigger. When he did, it needed to be pointed at Logan.

"Man, that's pretty messed up," Logan said. "But Miss Weslee didn't do anything, Josh. She does everything she can to nurture kids, and she'd never hurt anyone."

"My dad wants her. He hasn't shut up about her hair or her body or how sweet and innocent she is." Josh pressed the gun against Weslee's temple. "I was going to get to her first, ya know." He glared at Logan. "But then you showed up and screwed everything up!"

The lantern gave off enough light to let Logan see the madness in Josh's eyes. He needed that gun pointed at him before he could try to disarm the kid.

"Sorry, kid, but I don't think you're man enough for her," Logan said, taking a deliberate step forward.

His plan worked, and Josh aimed the gun at him, giving Logan the green light to rush him. Weslee screamed out his name as a deafening sound echoed from the gunshot. Logan had been shot at countless times as a SEAL, but he'd never once been hit. Until now. As the impact of bullet threw him backward, the only pain he felt was the knowledge that he'd failed to protect Weslee.

CHAPTER 15

*L*ogan!" Weslee screamed as she watched him fall to the ground. Where had the bullet hit him? Relief flooded her when he got to his knees and looked at Josh. Blood soaked through his T-shirt, giving her hope that the bullet had only grazed his shoulder.

"Why did you make me do that?" Josh yelled. The hand holding the gun shook violently, and he let go of Weslee to steady it with his other hand.

"Go!" Logan shouted at Weslee. "Now!"

Before Josh could grab her, she obeyed Logan. She didn't want to leave him but knew the only way she could help him was to get to a phone.

"Get back here!" Josh raged. Then another shot rang out.

She waited for the pain to hit her as she dove behind the pool table. Her breath came in short gasps as she realized he had missed. Then she heard a grunt of pain and knew he'd shot Logan again. *Please, don't let him die,* she silently prayed.

"You made me do that," Josh said, his voice bordering on a

sob. She wanted to hurt Robbie herself. What kind of man did that to his son? "I didn't want to kill anyone."

The air in Weslee's lung felt trapped as an iron fist of fear clenched around her throat and squeezed. Logan couldn't be dead.

"You need to come back over here, Weslee, if you don't want me to shoot your boyfriend again."

"Stay where you are," Logan groaned.

He's alive! Weslee thanked God as she dragged air into her lungs.

Josh swore at Logan and told him to shut up, but no shot followed the demand. Unfortunately, Logan didn't make another sound either. That's when Weslee knew it was up to her to save him.

Adrenaline surged through her, bathing her brain with a calmness incongruent with the rapid beating of her heart. Since her phone was still charging next to her bed, calling 9-1-1 wasn't an option. The chances of Inez waking were slim, which was probably for the best. Her nanny would die protecting Weslee.

She needed a weapon. It was the only way to possibly save Logan's life as well as her own. One of the balls from the pool table could work if her aim were as true as she shot an arrow.

An arrow. It was exactly what she needed. On the wall adjacent to the one at her back, her daddy had hung the plaque she'd won at her first archery tournament alongside the bow she'd used and at least one arrow. She couldn't remember if there were more, but one was all she needed.

Josh was muttering to himself about how much he hated his father and that his plans were all ruined. He was crying too, which broke her heart despite the revenge plan he'd concocted to get back at Robbie. Crawling on her hands and knees, Weslee slowly inched out from her hiding place. The room was dark except for the faint light from the lantern and Logan's flashlight. The storm raged on outside, but she remained calm.

"You need to come out, Weslee," Josh hollered in a scratchy voice. "I don't want to do it but y'all have left me no choice."

Didn't want to do what? Kill her? Her pulse accelerated, and she moved a little faster. She only had a couple more feet to go before she could get the bow and arrow down.

"There's always a choice, Josh," Logan said. His low voice filled Weslee with renewed hope. "It's not too late for you to make a good choice here." Logan then elaborated on what he thought of Robbie, using colorful expletives for emphasis. Although she'd never used that kind of language, she completely agreed with him.

"I told you to shut up!" Josh's voice resonated in the room, making Weslee start to shake. She had to get back in control if she wanted a chance to save Logan.

"Hey, I'm on your side," Logan said, ignoring the young man's demand that he stay quiet.

She saw Josh whirl around and lift the gun, pointing it exactly where Logan sat. From this vantage point, she could see Logan was still fully alert. Despite the shoulder wound, both his hands were pressed against his thigh. The bullet wound to his leg was the only reason Logan hadn't gotten to his feet, which might be the thing that saved his life, that is if he didn't die from blood loss. The beam from the flashlight was pointed in Logan's direction and she could see his pants were soaked with dark, red blood.

Josh raged on about his dad, using more swear words than Logan had used. She took advantage and slowly stood up. Her fingers connected with an arrow...no, two arrows. They were easy to remove. Once she had those locked under one arm, she lifted the bow from the wall. It scraped a little, but a synchronized gust of wind shook the windows and covered the sound.

"This is your last chance, Weslee," Josh yelled, keeping his eyes and gun trained on Logan. "Come back over here or I'm going to shoot your boyfriend. And this time I'll aim for his heart."

A fierce power surged through her like a jolt of lightning. Logan's heart belonged to her and nobody was going to shoot it. She nocked one of the arrows in place and took aim. Her hand trembled with raw emotions. As if her daddy were right here talking to her, she could almost hear his voice telling her to clear her mind and focus on the target.

"I'm counting to five, Weslee." He started the countdown, thankfully pausing between each number to give her the final edge she needed.

Drawing back the string, she zeroed in on the target and let the arrow fly just as Josh counted to number three. She remained poised as the arrow struck its mark. Josh screamed obscenities as the gun dropped to the floor with a thud. An arrow was stuck in his hand, right where she'd wanted it to go.

She already had the other arrow nocked when he turned toward her and bellowed in pain. He started running toward her. She didn't focus on what Logan was doing or the fact that in seconds Josh was going to plow into her. She took aim and let the arrow fly, striking him in the thigh. With another cry of pain, Josh went down. His head connected with a small marble table as he fell with a loud thud.

The lights flickered twice before staying on. Josh lay on the floor as if he were dead. She saw a goose egg the size of a golf ball forming on his temple, blood trickling down. He lay at an awkward angle, both arrows still buried in his flesh. As she approached him, she saw his chest rise and fall.

Her calm demeanor fled as quickly as the light's had come

back on. Adrenaline poured through her veins, and she nearly fell because her legs felt like noodles.

Logan had tried scooting toward the gun but didn't get very far. Not with the amount of blood pouring out of the bullet wound in his thigh. Their eyes connected as she stooped down and picked up the weapon. She knew how to handle a gun. And she knew she would use it if she had to.

"Did you shoot those arrows?" Logan asked. His face was pale, and his lips held very little color. It had to be a good sign that they weren't blue.

"I did," she said, moving quickly to his side. "Logan, you're losing so much blood."

He ignored her and gave her a roguish grin. "That was so hot," he said, his words sounding slurred as if he'd had too much to drink.

She rolled her eyes. If he could flirt with her then there was still hope. "Hang tight, and I'll get something to stop the bleeding."

"Yeah, I'm not going anywhere, sweetheart."

She was already on her feet and ran toward the kitchen. Thank goodness her daddy had insisted on a landline. Setting the gun on the countertop, she picked up the cordless phone and punched in 9-1-1 while she yanked open the drawer that held the dishtowels.

"9-1-1, what's your emergency?" a calm female voice said into her ear.

As she gave the woman the critical details, she grabbed the kitchen shears and rushed back to Logan's side. Putting the phone on speaker, she set it down next to her and made a few cuts in the fabric of the dishcloth and then ripped the white linen into several long strips. Inez had embroidered this set, but she knew she wouldn't care they were being torn apart.

"He's losing a lot of blood," Weslee told the dispatcher, not liking how quiet Logan was. She darted her eyes up to find him watching her, a small smile on his lips. Did that mean he was doing better than she thought or was he in shock and letting his guard down?

The dispatch operator ordered her to put a tourniquet on, giving her ideas of things she could use as Weslee slipped the first strip of cloth under Logan's injured leg. She'd taken a wilderness first-aid course before, but training for trauma and actually treating trauma were so different.

Her fingers were covered in sticky blood as she grabbed both ends of the cloth and started to tie them together. Logan was big but the old-fashioned dishtowels were longer and she was able to secure a tight knot. The operator reassured her that help was on the way as Weslee wadded up the remaining dishtowel and applied pressure to Logan's thigh.

"Did you go to combat-medic school or something?" he asked in a raspy voice. "You're good at this."

Ignoring him, she answered the dispatcher's question about the perpetrator. Weslee confirmed Josh was still unconscious by taking a quick look over her shoulder. She hoped he remained that way until help arrived. Of course, she didn't want him to die. She just didn't want him to wake up yet.

She heard the dispatcher ask for an ETA and then relayed that the paramedics should arrive in four minutes. That seemed like an eternity right now, but at least they were on their way.

"Weslee?" Logan said as she applied another layer of Inez's towels on top of the other one.

"Yes," she said, looking into his eyes. He seemed lucid. Until he spoke.

"In case I don't make it will you to tell me what your password was?"

"Stop talking," she said tersely. "The ambulance is on the way."

"I promise not to die if you tell me." His voice trailed off. "Please?" he added on.

"You're not going to die, Logan." Not if she had anything to do about it. She squeezed his hand. "Save your energy and focus on your breathing."

As usual, he ignored her. "Come on, babe. It's driving me crazy not knowing."

"Oh for heaven's sakes, Logan. It was HotNavyGuy."

He tried to give her that sexy smirk of his but didn't have the energy. He licked his lips that were now colorless. "Were you talking about me?" he asked in a sluggish tone that scared her to death.

"Yes, I was talking about you." She shook him when his eyelids started to drift closed. "Logan, you have to stay awake."

"Can't." She saw him try to swallow. "Too tired."

"Please," she said, tears welling in her eyes. "Please, stay awake. I love you and I can't lose you too."

That got his attention, and he opened his eyes. "You really do love me?"

"Yes, and I want to marry you and have babies with you and fly in a helicopter with you and climb mountains with you and eat cookie dough with you and— "

"Hey, babe," he said, closing his eyes again. "Gonna have to talk about this later. I don't feel so good." Logan's head fell to the side as his body gave up trying to stay awake.

"WHERE ARE THEY?" she shrieked at the dispatch operator. "He's dying!"

"Ma'am, I need you to remain calm and tell me if the patient is still breathing."

"Yes! But they need to hurry!" She was prepared to start CPR and began going over the steps in her mind.

The cavalry arrived moments later. She'd never been so happy to see someone and wanted to hug the two police officers that rushed through the door. With their guns drawn, one of the men rushed over to Josh while the other one asked about the location of the weapon the shooter used.

"I put it on the countertop." Weslee knew why he wanted to locate the gun, but she wanted help for Logan. "Where is the ambulance? He's losing too much blood."

"They're here, ma'am," he said, as he located the gun on the countertop.

If they were here then where were they! Before Weslee shouted out the question, the police officer spoke into his mic, stating the scene was clear and safe to enter.

Paramedics arrived seconds later, and Weslee got out of the way so one of the medics could take her place. "I need a line, STAT," he said to his partner while at the same time checked Logan's pulse. "Let's get an IO in him and start fluids," he ordered as he put an oxygen mask over Logan's nose and mouth. Then she watched him put on a much more substantial tourniquet than the one she'd made from a dishtowel.

More first responders arrived and immediately went to check on Josh when the cop called out for a medic to assist him. Weslee was too frightened by everything they were doing to Logan to find out any details on Josh.

While one paramedic cut the lower pant leg to Logan's uninjured limb, the other one cut off his T-shirt. She didn't have time to appreciate his sculpted chest as the man affixed heart monitor leads to his skin, but she was relieved to see the gunshot wound to the shoulder wasn't bleeding very much. Meanwhile, the second paramedic shaved a section of hair from Logan's lower leg, wiped the patch of skin with a pad that left an orange stain, and used a drill to insert the IV access directly through the shin bone. Logan didn't even flinch.

As the paramedic hung a bag of IV fluids, he asked dispatch for an ETA on the emergency helicopter. Weslee didn't remember anyone calling for a helicopter. It made sense though since there was only a small urgent care facility on the island.

All at once a wave of nausea hit her, and she nearly toppled over, even though she sat poised on her knees. In a haze of dizziness, she saw neighbors had gathered near the open door. She saw Robbie and heard him cry out Josh's name.

The last thing she remembered was somebody shouting that she was going down before everything went dark.

CHAPTER 16

*L*ogan's eyelids had to be glued down because he couldn't open them no matter how hard he tried. If he didn't know better he'd think Jace had pranked him. Voices echoed in his head, sounding loud and then soft as if someone was screwing around with the volume on a radio.

He must be dreaming because he could hear Jace's voice talking with Weslee.

Weslee. The thought of her set off a chain reaction as events slammed through his head. It was like a PowerPoint slideshow gone berserk. He wanted to cuss out whoever was doing it and tell them to start over so he could make sense of the images.

"I think he's waking up," a soft feminine voice said with a southern drawl. He felt a hand slide into his, and he knew it was Weslee. He tried to squeeze her hand, but nothing worked.

"Yes," another woman's voice said, sounding exactly like his mother. "He's trying to open his eyes.

"I'll go find his nurse," a man said. "The cute one, not the mean one." That voice definitely belonged to Jace. Logan tried to make a sarcastic comment to his friend, but it was like his brain and his mouth didn't connect.

"Just remember to send someone in, please," his mother said with a laugh.

"Yes, ma'am," Jace responded.

Mom. Mom. Logan tried forming the word, but all he got out was a moan.

"Logan, honey, it's okay." It was his mom again, and he felt her fingers wrap around his other hand. "You're just fine, sweet boy."

Sweet boy? He was either having a wicked nightmare or he'd come close to dying for his mother to call him a *sweet boy*.

He asked what had happened to him. He must have actually spoken the words aloud and inserted a few swear words because his mother reprimanded him. "Logan, you don't want to scare off your beautiful girlfriend with that kind of language."

"He can't scare me off," Weslee said with a soft laugh. "But I may have to make him start paying me money or something every time he curses."

"Is that my boy swearing like a sailor?" Jace asked. "Good, that means his brain didn't sustain any damage."

Logan said something to Jace about his brain being the damaged one. His comment must have come out wrong because his mother squeezed his hand. "Logan, for goodness sake, son. You need to wake up before they have to censure your hospital room."

"Stop being so naughty," that southern voice whispered in his ear. "And open your eyes and look at me."

He did as she commanded.

Logan blinked against the bright light as Jace snorted a laugh. "And another single-man bites the dust." His friend came into focus at the end of his bed. It wasn't the face he was looking for. "Looks like I'm planning a funeral after all," Jace snickered.

"Jace Burns," his mother scolded. "I swear I need to send you and Logan to a boot camp for manners."

"Sorry, ma'am," Jace said, sounding anything but sorry.

"Sorry, Mom," Logan said, knowing his tongue was loose because of the meds. He usually had a better filter than this, but words just kept popping in his mind and slipping out of his mouth. He slid his eyes over to see his mom's beautiful face. "Wow, Mom, you look really pretty with a tan."

"Don't try sweet talkin' me, young man. Save that for your girlfriend." She smiled at him and winked. "By the way, I really like her," she whispered in a way that wasn't really a whisper. "Pain meds or not, you behave, or I really will ground you."

"Yes, ma'am." Then he turned his head, and his gaze collided with the most beautiful light blue eyes. "Hi, girlfriend," he said, trying to lift his hand from the bed. He wanted to wrap it around her neck and bring her mouth down to his.

"Hey," Weslee said with a tiny hiccup. Tears welled in her eyes, making the color shimmer like a cove in the Caribbean Sea.

A memory flitted across his groggy brain. He chased after the memory and caught it as he recalled her shooting a bow and arrow that knocked the gun from the kid's hand.

"You shot an arrow to save my life, right?"

"Yes."

He gave a low whistle. "Man, that was so hot."

"So you said before," Weslee said with a light laugh.

Jace guffawed loudly while his mother groaned out loud that she'd failed as a mother. But Weslee...she just curved those perfect lips up into the sexiest smile he'd ever seen, sending a rush of heat through his body.

"Hey, can you bring that pretty mouth a little closer?" he asked Weslee. "I really want to kiss your right now."

That earned him another groan from his mother. He could hear Jace snickering in the background. "I'm posting this to YouTube," he said. "It's gonna go viral and make me a lot of money."

He didn't pay much attention because Weslee had obeyed him. She leaned in, and he caught the fresh scent of her hair. "I must really love you," she said, her mouth close but not close enough, "if I'm about to kiss a man who has had his teeth brushed with a pink, minty sponge for the past two days."

"You really love me?" he asked, almost positive they'd had this conversation before.

"Yes, Lieutenant Steele. I really do." Logan wanted to tell her not to kiss him until he at least chewed a piece of gum, but the second her lips brushed his mouth he forgot all about it.

The kiss ended before he could respond and kiss her properly. "Hey, that wasn't a very good kiss."

Jace busted a gut, which covered up his mom's sound of dismay.

"I promise to give you a much better one later," Weslee said, kissing him on his cheek. "Besides, your doctor's here now."

The room quieted and Logan tried concentrating on what the doctor was saying as the man talked about how lucky Logan was to have had someone as smart as Weslee with him. Apparently, she'd saved his life twice that day. First with the arrows and then by tying a tourniquet around his leg and applying pressure to the gunshot wound.

"You'd already lost a fair amount of blood from the flesh wound to the shoulder, but the bullet nicked an artery in your thigh," the doctor continued. "You would've bled out by the time the paramedics arrived if Miss Weslee hadn't acted promptly and waited for them to help you."

As the doctor talked about his recovery period, Logan sought out Weslee's face. She was listening to the doctor so intently. He wanted her to look at him. He squeezed her hand, pleased he could actually follow through with the motion.

She shifted her attention to him and the look in her eyes made his throat feel like he'd swallowed a chunk of bread whole. She loved him. He could see in her eyes as if she'd spoken the words out loud again.

He blinked as a memory flashed in his mind. It was of her finally telling him the password to her computer. Other memories bounced in front of his eyes and then back out. She'd said a lot of other things to him. He just couldn't grab a hold of what they were.

"What else did you tell me when I was dying?" he asked her in a hushed voice, trying not to disrupt the doctor.

"Shh," Weslee said. "The doctor's not done. We can talk in a minute."

It was driving him crazy that he couldn't remember what else she'd said to him. He would just talk quieter. "Just whisper so they don't hear," Logan said, pointing to his mom and the doctor.

Jace snorted a laugh and then covered it with a fake cough.

His mom sighed dramatically. "I'm sorry, Dr. Andrews. My son isn't normally this rude. The medication is making him loopy, and he's a little distracted right now, but I'm listening to every word you have to say."

"I think I might be distracted too, Mrs. Steele," Dr. Andrews said with a hearty chuckle. "I'll check back in when I make rounds this evening." He smiled and gave Logan's good shoulder a fatherly pat. "Let your nurse know if you need anything."

"Yes, sir," Logan said, giving the man a salute. Then he shifted his gaze to Weslee. Man, she was prettier than he'd remembered. He watched her smile at the doctor and thank him before the man left the room.

"You're so beautiful," he said when she finally looked at him.

"I'm not sure if that's you or the meds talking," she said with a smirk.

He blinked a couple of times. "Nope, you're still really pretty."

"Ah, man," Jace said. "My phone just died."

Then, as if someone had just inserted a flash drive in Logan's brain, he recalled every word Weslee had said to him. "You want to have babies with me?" he asked, that one sentence sticking out in the forefront.

"Good Lord," his mother prayed out loud. "Please tell me where I went wrong."

"Mama Steele," Jace snickered. "I think we better leave these two alone."

"I think you're right. Besides, Miss Inez and Mr. Curtis are on their way back. We can give these two some privacy while updating the others on everything." His mom's face hovered over his. "Behave yourself, Logan Steele," she said again, brushing a kiss to his forehead. "I really like her."

Weslee pulled up a chair next to the bed, still holding his hand while she did it. It was just the two of them now. "So," he said, giving her a wry grin, "do you want to have babies with me?"

Her smile was a slow lift of the lips. "Are you tellin' me out of everything I said to you that's the only part you remember?"

"Uh, yeah," he said, accidentally slipping in a mild curse word. He was a guy. Of course, that's the part he'd recall first. "Sorry about swearing. I swear I'll work on cleaning up my language."

That made her laugh. He loved her laugh. Oh, man, he loved her.

"I love you, Weslee," he said, his voice husky with emotion. He'd always been so afraid to utter those words to any woman, which was kind of ironic for a former Navy SEAL whose job description required courage and bravery as a prerequisite. At least the girl he'd fallen in love with was fearless enough to tell him first. Only right now she looked completely astounded by his declaration. "You still love me, right?" he asked, lifting one eyebrow.

She answered him with a soft kiss that, once again, didn't last long enough. "I love you, too, Logan," she said, pulling back before he could lift his hand to keep her close.

His eyes skimmed over her face. A face he loved and wanted to see every night before he went to sleep and first thing in the morning. He'd almost died, and his second chance at life wasn't going to be spent worrying about things he couldn't control. Time was a precious thing, and he didn't want to waste one second away from Weslee.

He wished he had some piece of jewelry he could give her because he wanted to ask her to marry him right now. Then he remembered his bracelets. He looked at his wrist, but they weren't there.

"They had to cut them off in the helicopter. You needed more fluids, and they had to start another IV." She squeezed his hand and then let go and stood up. "The nurse gave them to me to keep safe for you." She rummaged around in her purse and found what she'd been looking for.

"May I see them?" he asked. "Please?"

"Yes." She walked back to the chair and sat down. "But first you need to chew on this, sailor." She placed a square piece of gum against his lips and then slipped it in with her fingers.

Dang, he had no idea how hot it could be to have a girl feed him. He definitely needed to put a ring on her finger. "Wow, thank you," he said, chewing the gum in hopes of getting the much better kiss she'd promised sooner than later.

"Oh, it's gonna be my pleasure," she teased with a sultry wink that spiked Logan's core body temperature to the point of spontaneous combustion. "Don't you dare tell your mama I said that," Weslee said with a laugh. "I couldn't help it. After spending so much time with Jace I think his sense of humor has rubbed off on me."

Logan narrowed his eyes. "He didn't try to steal you away, did he?"

"Several times, but I told him I have eyes for only one Hot Navy Guy."

"You think he's hot?"

"Goodness, Logan, did you hear anything else I said?"

"You have eyes only for me?"

"Exactly." She sobered a bit as she handed him the two string bracelets. "They were careful and cut them in a way you can re-tie them if you want."

He rubbed the two strings with his thumb and finger, feeling the familiar edge. "I do want to re-tie them." He shifted on the bed. "Does this bed raise up a little?"

She pushed a button that raised the head of the bed up so he was no longer staring up at her. "Better?" she asked.

"Much." He held her gaze for a heartbeat before focusing on one of the bracelets, folding it over a few times to shorten the string.

When he was satisfied, he looked at her and held out his hand with his palm up. She placed her left hand in his, which was the one he wanted. Bringing her hand to his mouth, he kissed her fingers, saving her ring finger for last. Letting go, he picked up the shortened string and carefully tied it around her left ring finger.

"Logan," she said in a shaky voice. "What're you doin'?"

He gave her a crooked smile. "I promise I'll get you a better ring, but this one will have to do for now."

"A better ring?" she asked as her lower lip started to quiver.

"Weslee Anne Campbell." He winked at her. "Learned your middle name when I ordered my stuff from Ground Zero." He'd forgotten all about the order and hoped it was still on his doorstep. "Weslee Anne Campbell," he said again. "I think I fell in love with you that day on the beach when you ran into me."

She captured her quivering lip with her upper teeth, her eyes glistening with unshed tears. She seemed to cry easily, but if she could put up with him then he could tolerate her tears.

"I was too stupid to ask for your name and number."

"I wouldn't have given it to you, anyway," she teased.

He grinned. Being married to her was going to be a lot of fun. She better say yes.

"I did come back a few times, hoping to run into you again. And then I walked into Sutton's conference room and saw you sitting there."

He knew she could razz him about thinking Jon was the one he was supposed to protect, but she didn't.

"Let's just say I knew that my life was about to change forever." He swallowed and ran his thumb over the string on her finger. "That is if you'll have mercy on me and be my wife?"

A small laugh bubbled out of her. "Yes! Yes, I'll be your wife." She sniffed. "And I don't want a better ring. I love this one." She held it up and admired it like it was a two-carat diamond. "I'm never taking it off."

"Um, you've met my mother. I will buy you another ring." He motioned for her to come closer. "I think we should kiss now, don't you?"

Her enthusiastic *yes* was preceded with a mild curse word a preacher might use in a Sunday sermon. "And don't you dare tell your mother I said that either," she whispered with a teasing glint in her eyes.

His laughter was silenced when her mouth met his in a kiss that burned through him. He loved this girl so much, and he couldn't wait to marry her. "We're having a short engagement," he said against her mouth.

"A very short one," she said before giving him another kiss that was bound to set off his heart monitor.

Feeling his strength as well as a clearer mind return, Logan took over and kissed her long and slow, savoring the taste of her. He hadn't planned on this happening to him—falling in love—ever. But nothing had ever felt more right.

Their lips parted, and she edged back to gaze into his eyes. Shoot, courage and bravery had nothing to do with loving this girl. Having babies with her? That didn't scare him either, not with this beautiful woman by his side.

EPILOGUE

Six Weeks Later

*T*urning around, Weslee faced the full-length mirror and stared at her image. The bride gazing back at her looked as radiant as she felt inside. She smoothed a hand over the lacy white material of the floor-length skirt. She had fallen in love with the dress the moment she saw it. The lacy bodice had a high neckline and cap sleeves with a teardrop-shaped cutout in the back. The dress was seamless and hugged her body perfectly, making her feel like a princess.

"Oh, Weslee," Julia Steele said with a slight wobble in her voice. "You are the most beautiful bride." Logan's mother dabbed the corner of her eyes with a white hankie. "I don't know how my son found you, but I thank the Lord he did."

"Amen to that," Inez said, handing Weslee her wedding bouquet made up of yellow roses, tiny white daisies, and vibrant green leaves. "You truly are beautiful, baby girl. Logan won't be able to take his eyes off of you."

Weslee gave them a watery smile, willing herself not to cry.

Her makeup was perfect. The dress was perfect. This day was perfect because in approximately five minutes Uncle Jon would walk her down the aisle and give her away to Logan. The only thing that would make this better would be to have her parents here. Still, she felt them close by and knew they were happy for her.

"Thank you, ma'am," she said, giving Julia's hand a squeeze. "I feel like the luckiest girl in the world to be marrying him."

Tears formed in Julia's eyes that were similar to the color of her son's. "Remember I want you to call me mom," she said. "Because I already think of you like the daughter I've always wanted."

"You two need to stop this," Inez said wiping at the corner of her eye. "You'll mess up your makeup, Weslee, and delay the wedding." Inez handed her a clean tissue. "And we all know that groom of yours will not be happy about a delay."

"No, he won't," Weslee said with a laugh.

Her soon-to-be-husband hadn't been kidding about having a short engagement. He'd wanted to get married the day after he was released from the hospital. His mother insisted on two months. Inez voted for three months. Jon voted on a year, which everyone shot down quite vehemently. Especially Logan, who hadn't had a problem with bad language since the effects of the IV pain meds had worn off while he was in the hospital. However, he'd had a slight relapse when Jon suggested the year-long wait.

It was already torturing enough for them to say goodbye each night. She couldn't imagine postponing much longer.

In the end, Weslee convinced Logan to give her at least six weeks. It wasn't easy and required a lot of promises she intended to keep—just as soon as they were husband and wife.

Glancing at the wall clock, Weslee was suddenly hit with a

bout of nerves. "Logan is here, right?" she asked, placing a hand over her stomach.

Looking at one another, Inez and Julia both started laughing.

"Honey, that boy couldn't possibly get cold feet," Inez said a moment later. "He's like a walking inferno, especially when y'all are together."

"He's here, sweetheart," Julia said tenderly. "And still grumbling about having to wait until this evening."

"I know." Weslee smiled, thinking about the text message she'd received from him at 0500 asking her why they couldn't be married during a sunrise instead of waiting for the sun to set. "But he knows why this time is important to me."

Truthfully, the timing was just as important to Logan. They'd chosen to be married on the beach in San Diego where they'd first run into each other, keeping the same timeframe too, which was just before sunset. All of his former SEAL team had arrived hours ago to help the wedding planner set up chairs for the guests as well as the pretty archway she and Logan would stand under while they pledged their lives together.

The wedding party wasn't large. They'd wanted the ceremony to be simple, but she'd quickly learned just how tight Logan and his SEAL team were. She now felt like she had five older brothers. Annoying brothers sometimes, but oh so loyal. They'd do anything for Logan and for her now.

Jace was Logan's best man. Creed, Baron, Maddox, and Blaine were all groomsmen. Weslee had asked Kate to be her maid of honor. The two of them had become good friends, continuing to go to the spa together at least twice a week after Weslee had relocated to San Diego. She'd taken up residence in her parent's oceanfront house when Logan had been released from the hospital. Only now she was in the large master bedroom on the first floor, anxiously waiting for Logan to move in with her.

She and Logan had decided to make their home in San Diego for now. She would commute to North Carolina as needed until the new CEO Jon had hired took over Ground Zero. While she would maintain her shares in the company, she wanted her focus to be more on running the charities her parents had devoted most of their time to. Then, once she and Logan started a family, she could pick and choose how her time was spent.

Moving to California didn't mean she was ready to sever her ties with North Carolina. She loved the memories she had with her parents and didn't want them tainted by what had happened on Emerald Isle. After talking it over with Logan, she decided to sell the beach house as well as her parent's mansion outside of Raleigh. They wanted a fresh start and a chance to create new memories in their own beach house. Eventually, they planned on building a vacation home somewhere on the East Coast. As much as she loved Emerald Isle, she couldn't imagine going back. The community was small, and she knew returning there would make the Whitakers uncomfortable. They were already suffering enough from the events that nearly took Logan's life.

Hopefully, staying away would also give Robbie and Josh a chance to mend their relationship as Josh received the mental health care he needed while serving out his sentence in juvenile detention. Since he was still a minor and Logan hadn't died, the kid had been given a break. Both Weslee and Logan hoped the young man could make something of his life. They also hoped Robbie would get the help he needed too. It turned out that he did have a drinking problem. The whole incident with Josh's girlfriend had happened when he was drunk, and he claimed he didn't remember much about it or that Josh had known.

"Miss Inez?" Kate called from the large walk-in closet. "Could you help me get the zipper?"

"I knew she'd need help," Inez whispered.

"I heard that," Kate said. "And I'm not opposed to asking for help if I need it."

Inez rolled her eyes and hurried to help the maid of honor. Kate was fiercely independent and didn't rely on anyone if she didn't have to. Raised in foster care, Kate had learned that if she wanted something out of life then she had to do it for herself. She'd had a hard time letting go of the belief that trusting someone and asking for help didn't mean she was weak.

A knock sounded at the door, sending a rush of adrenaline through Weslee. That had to be Jon because Logan wouldn't have knocked, just barged right in.

"Hello, Jon," Julia said when she opened the door. "You look very handsome."

"Thank you, Julia," he said as color infused his face. "You look absolutely beautiful."

Weslee bit back a smile as she watched the couple with tenderness. The two of them had become good friends when Logan was in the hospital, but something had shifted in their relationship the past few weeks. There was definitely a spark between them.

Logan hadn't liked it at first, but after seeing his mom with adult eyes rather than his boyhood perspective, he had changed his mind. He and his mom had finally openly talked about his father's death and how it had affected both of their lives. His mom admitted that her grief had been so overwhelming that she never wanted to marry again. She felt bad that she hadn't adequately followed up with Logan as her heart had healed. She wasn't opposed to marrying again, she'd just never found anyone to fall in love with again. To be fair, Logan hadn't made talking about it easy. The two of them had fallen into a pattern of avoiding the subject.

Jon's gaze landed on Weslee. "What a beautiful bride you are, Weslee my girl," he said, walking over to give her a kiss on the cheek. "Are you ready for this?"

"More than ready," she said. It was past time she married her Hot Navy Guy.

"Good, because I've got six Navy SEALs breathing down my neck to come and get the bride or they are going to do it their way." He wiped his forehead with a handkerchief. "I don't even want to know what their way entails."

"Probably not," Weslee said with a giggle. Logan had told her at least five different ways he could get in and out of the house with her and no one would even know he'd been there.

She believed him. Last week, he and Jace had gone on a special ops mission they'd said was confidential. However, a few days later, Jon miraculously found a file sitting on his desk with information about Dax Hamilton stealing company secrets, as well as proof that he'd altered his contract with Ground Zero by removing the non-compete clause.

Weslee had known exactly where the file had come from, but when she confronted Logan about it, he'd just grinned and told her that the information was classified and that she didn't have the proper security clearance.

It had only taken a few persuasive kisses to get him to admit he and Jace had let themselves into Dax's house to look for incriminating evidence. They claimed it wasn't breaking and entering since technically they didn't break anything.

"Let's get this show on the road," Kate said as she and Inez entered the room. She looked beautiful in the ice-blue dress Weslee had picked out for her friend. "Wow," Kate said, stopping in front of Weslee. "You look so gorgeous I might consider doing this someday."

Her comment was progress. Kate vehemently swore that marriage wasn't for her. Weslee was just waiting for the day when her friend met her match.

"Thank you." Weslee handed her maid of honor a small bouquet of white and yellow daisies. "You look beautiful, Kate. The single guys Logan invited are going to be fighting over you."

"Oh please," Kate said. "That's funny considering I could probably kick all of their butts."

"Ladies," Jon said. "Logan is going to break down this door if we don't get going."

That got everyone moving. Inez and Julia left to find their seats. Then the music started and Kate preceded Weslee down the pathway that was lined with rows of flickering lanterns on both sides. As soon as Weslee stepped onto the start of the makeshift path, the wedding coordinator cued the music for the bride. An acoustic instrumental version of Ed Sheeran's *Perfect* started playing. It was the song Weslee and Logan had danced to at the charity ball and shared their first kiss to.

The audience rose, but Weslee had eyes for only her groom. The awed expression on his face melted her heart, and she had to check the impulse to break out into a run to get to him quicker.

***

Logan stared at his beautiful bride as a wave of emotions slammed into him. His eyes stung and, for the first time that he could remember as an adult, he felt like crying. He didn't, but a burning sensation pressed against the back of his eyes and his chest tightened as love for this woman filled every part of him.

"Dang, she looks beautiful," Jace said under his breath. "You're one lucky son of a gun."

Logan couldn't agree more. He felt bad about ever giving his married friends grief about handing over their man card to tie themselves down to a woman. Giving his heart to Weslee was the best decision he'd ever made.

His eyes locked with hers, and she curved her lips into a soft and sexy smile as if she could read his thoughts. He smiled back, not caring if everyone present saw how much he loved her. It's not that he'd tried hiding his feelings, he had just grown very impatient with only telling her how much he loved her. Waiting to show her how he felt about her had been difficult, but he loved her too much to push for more.

The wound in his thigh twitched, reminding him of how close he'd come to dying. Thinking of it still had the power to humble him. Without Weslee's actions that day, he would've died. The amount of blood loss for a man his size had been significant. The trauma surgeon had estimated Logan had lost forty percent of his blood volume and had been minutes away from his heart stopping. He hated to think about missing out on a life with Weslee, especially as her husband.

The walk down the pathway seemed to take forever. Finally, she was near enough he could hold out his hand. Euphoria washed over him as she placed her hand in his. "Hi, beautiful," he whispered as he lifted her hand to his mouth and pressed a lingering kiss to her knuckles, all the while maintaining eye contact with her.

"Hello, handsome," she whispered back.

He knew he wasn't supposed to kiss her yet, but he couldn't help it. Grinning, he pulled her to him and kissed her soundly on the mouth. The audience chuckled, and he heard his mother mutter that her son never did anything the conventional way.

Cannon, a former SEAL and Navy chaplain, cleared his throat. Logan and Weslee drew apart and faced the man who had the authority to make them husband and wife. Cannon grinned and addressed everyone in attendance. "I guess since these two are anxious to get to the kissing part, I'll have to skip the lengthy oration I had planned."

"My future husband and I appreciate that very much," Weslee said, making Cannon, the wedding party and the audience all laugh.

Logan was tempted to lay another kiss on her sassy mouth when Cannon started the ceremony by welcoming everyone. "We are gathered here in this special setting to celebrate the love between Weslee and Logan, by joining them in marriage."

Although he tried to listen to each word spoken by the chaplain, Logan was distracted by his beautiful bride. With Cannon's prompting, they each repeated their vows. Then it was time to exchange rings. As much as Weslee loved the ring he'd made from one of his bracelets, it wasn't practical. His mom had come up with an idea of how to preserve them. She'd taken both of the bracelets and had them framed along with a quote by Thomas Jefferson that talked about the price of freedom. It now hung on the wall of the bedroom he would soon share with Weslee.

Jace nudged Logan and handed him the ring. Logan had designed the diamond ring himself. He'd wanted Weslee's ring to be as unique and special as she was. Without a doubt, he knew she was the only one for him. His hands were surprisingly steady as he slipped the one-of-a-kind ring onto his bride's finger, repeating the words that bound them together.

After Weslee slipped his ring on, Cannon finally pronounced them husband and wife. "Now, you may kiss your bride," he said to Logan.

As the crowd clapped and cheered, Logan held Weslee's face in his hands and touched her lips softly, reveling in the feel of his wife's silky mouth. *My wife.* Just the thought that she was finally his sent his pulse skittering. Remembering they had an audience, he checked the banked passion that begged him to deepen the kiss.

"We'll finish this later," he murmured against her lips. After giving her one last tender kiss, he drew back and swooped her up in his arms. "Let's get this party started," he said, carrying his wife down the pathway.

His groomsmen all hooted their approval as the DJ started the playlist he and Jace had come up with. The reception was set up on the back terrace and pool deck of their house. The food was delicious, but it was the chocolate chip cookie dough that was the most popular. Logan even caught Inez tasting the specially made dessert that was safe to eat since it didn't contain any raw eggs.

The celebration was amazing, but Logan was anxious to get his wife alone. They planned to leave soon after their first dance as husband and wife. Until that time, he and Weslee made the rounds, visiting with each guest. They posed for wedding photos, cut the cake and then it was time. As the DJ asked the crowd to clear the dance floor for the bride and groom's first dance as husband and wife, Logan led Weslee to the center of the floor. He didn't bother with a formal dance hold, wanting her as close to him as possible.

"I love you," he said, gazing into her eyes as they slowly swayed to the original soundtrack of *Perfect.*

"I love you, too." She fingered the hair of his neck and gave him a secretive smile that hinted at things to come. "I can't believe we're really married."

"I can't believe you made me wait so long."

"Good things come to those that wait," she said, giving him that smile again.

"I'm glad you brought that up," Logan said as the song neared the end. "What about those wedding-date negotiations?" Now that they were married, he felt like it was only fair that she told him a little more about the promises she'd made to him.

A spark of mischief flickered in her eyes. "Sorry, Lieutenant Steele, but that's classified information."

Giving her a roguish smile, Logan leaned down and brushed his lips over hers. "There's one thing you forgot, Mrs. Steele," he murmured against her mouth.

"Oh?" she whispered back.

"I now have security clearance."

She giggled softly as Logan caught her mouth in a kiss, his lips moving tenderly over hers with thorough deliberation. The sweet scent of her skin flooded his senses as Weslee pulled back, wrapped her arms around his neck, and whispered something only he was authorized to hear.

Logan's breath stilled and then he laughed, knowing his life would never be the same, except this time the thought didn't scare him. Sweeping her up into his arms, he kissed her again as he carried her off the dance floor. Good things do come to those who wait, and she was definitely worth the wait.

FREE BOOK

Thank you so much for reading The Rogue Warrior. If you liked, I hope you'll consider leaving a review for it on Amazon and GoodReads. I'm excited about the books I have coming out. Another book in November and more in 2019! If you'd like to receive updates on my books, as well as notices about new releases and sales on books from authors like me, please sign up for my Newsletter and receive a FREE copy of Catching Caytie just for signing up.

Thank you again for reading my books! My readers are the best and make writing worth it.

All the best,
Cindy

ALSO BY CINDY ROLAND ANDERSON

Individual Titles

Fair Catch

Discovering Sophie

Georgia Moon Romance Series

Under a Georgia Moon

Just a Kiss in the Moonlight

Blue Moon Kisses

Snow Valley Romance Series

An Unexpected Kiss

Catching Caytie

Operation Kiss the Girl

Destiny Came Knocking

Caught Kissing the Cowboy

Country Brides & Cowboy Boots Series

The Cowboy's Accidental Bride

Navy SEAL Romances 2.0

The Rogue Warrior

Under the Mistletoe: A Timeless Romance Anthology

Forgotten Kisses

ABOUT THE AUTHOR

Cindy Roland Anderson is an Amazon best-selling author who writes clean, contemporary romance with a combination of humor, romantic tension and some pretty great kissing scenes. She and her husband live in northern Utah, and are parents to five children, and grandparents to seven adorable grandchildren. She is a registered nurse and has worked in the NICU as well as the newborn nursery. She loves to read, almost as much as she loves writing. And she loves chocolate... probably a little too much. Be sure and sign up for Cindy's Newsletter and receive a free copy of one of her books. You'll also get notified first of her latest book release and the chance to receive an advanced copy of that new book before anyone else.

To see all her works please visit Cindy Roland Anderson's Author Page

Cindy loves to hear from her readers! To notify her please visit her website http://www.cindyrolandanderson.com

CPSIA information can be obtained
at www.ICGtesting.com
Printed in the USA
LVHW011607310119
605946LV00019B/639/P